Lessons in Husbandry

BY THE SAME AUTHOR:
Not a Fairytale (2010)

Lessons
in
Husbandry

SHAIDA KAZIE ALI

UMUZI

Published in 2012 by Umuzi
an imprint of Random House Struik (Pty) Ltd
Company Reg No. 1966/003153/07
First Floor, Wembley Square, Solan Road, Cape Town, 8001, South Africa
PO Box 1144, Cape Town, 8000, South Africa
umuzi@randomstruik.co.za
www.randomstruik.co.za

First edition, first printing 2012
1 3 5 7 9 8 6 4 2

ISBN 978-1-4152-0139-8 (PRINT)
ISBN 978-1-4152-0472-6 (ePub)
ISBN 978-1-4152-0473-3 (PDF)

Cover design by publicide
Text design by Chérie Collins
Author photograph by Gabeba Baderoon
Set in 13 on 17 pt Garamond Pro
Printed and bound in South Africa by
Interpak Books, Pietermaritzburg

To my mother, Haidr and Azhar

lesson, *n.* something to learn through good
or bad experience
husbandry, *n.* wise management
and care of private affairs

Contents

Prologue

Amal, this is the time of the year when I miss you most of all, as the days grow warmer and our birthdays draw closer. Today, that yearning feels new, as though it's a fresh sorrow. I know the reason for my sadness: it's the words skinny-dipping on the pages in front of me.

Don't laugh, when I tell you this is my memoir. I know it sounds pretentious, and, no, in your absence I haven't become a celebrity. I'm not a sex-fiend sports star, or a recovering drug addict or even a woman who spent a few dark hours with a famous married man. The memoir-writing course was Rakel's idea. She's my partner in our business, Celestial Cupcakes, and also my friend. She's been through a lot in her seventy-something years, so it seems sensible that she'd want to write an autobiography. But as with most of her ventures, she insisted I join her, and, as usual, I didn't argue, living, as I did then, on the outskirts of my life.

So that's why I'm here at my favourite coffee haunt in Cape Town, watching the sun spill over the pages as I read through my manuscript and wait for my husband to join me. I've decided that the easiest thing to do is to let him read what I've written. I don't know how he'll react, so I don't know how this story is going to end, and that is contributing to this melancholy I can't shake.

There's a breeze blowing in my direction, bringing with it a whiff of sea air, but I can still feel a slippery layer of sweat supergluing my spine to my dress (purple cotton, sleeveless, ankle length, for TALL women, says the label), which in turn has bonded with the café's wrought-iron chair, making us the beast with several legs. If I clambered onto the chair, I might be able to catch a glimpse of the ocean down in the hollow of the town's pit. That's if it were a clear day, but today the city is hazy, already blanketed by an early holiday-season hangover.

I'm trying not to be a clumsy narrator, Amal, but I don't know where to begin. I wish I could capture that first second when I knew you were gone, or even the memory of that original moment, and pin it to the page like a dead butterfly. But I can't. I only know that for a long time nothing happened, and then everything did. So here goes. I'll begin with the dedication.

For my sister, Amal.

You see, when I started writing this story, almost a year ago, my writing teacher told us to think of a person to dedicate our book to, to imagine that person as our ideal reader, someone who would read our words with compassion and generosity. I'm sure that's exactly how you'll read them, Amal, wherever you are.

How to Design a Memory Quilt

Alice stands in front of us, unassuming in a white shirt, blue denims and bare feet, exposing glossy toenails. Her hair has streaks of grey in it, like mine, but hers is blonde and cut into short feathery layers to match her owl spectacles. You'll be horrified to hear that I still wear my hair in a teacher-bun, or a single plait down my back.

Alice says, "Memoirs entice readers with their truths, whether these are factual accounts or the vaguest of memories that you recreate from pictures in your mind."

It's all very well for her to talk about truths, but if I were to tell the truth, I wouldn't be able to let anyone read this. Except for you, Amal.

"To write the story well, you need to find the emotional truth of your narrative and bring it alive for your reader through smells, textures and rhythms."

I look around at the other women in the class. There are six of us. I keep glancing at the woman sitting across the round table from me because she looks like Ursula the Sea Witch from *The Little Mermaid*, except for her hair, which is black and curly. She is wearing a long sombre dress with a trailing purple scarf.

Alice's writing room is above the bookstore she owns, which is attached to a coffee shop. I can't decide which is more seductive, the perfume of the coffee or the fragrance of the new books, which beg to be read each time I walk by them on my way to the writing room.

Alice's voice draws me back to the room. "It's time to introduce ourselves."

The Sea Witch rubs her hands together as if she's standing in front of an imaginary fire. The movement causes dozens of silver bangles and bracelets to jangle loudly. They loop around her arms like the annual circles you find inside trees. Maybe if I counted them I'd be able to determine her age.

"Me first, me first," she says, which means I can stop trying to avoid eye contact with Alice.

"I'm Clarissa," she says. "You might recognise me?"

No one speaks.

"From TV. *All My Pretty Ones?*"

There are murmurs of assent. I overhear "soapie". I don't watch soapies, only mysteries.

"I'm sure you all know it. I play Sylvia. But before that I was a stage actress and a movie star, so I've got many, many stories to tell."

She draws a hand up to replace a stray curl and the bangles on her arm jingle like the tinny bells on cats' collars.

"In fact, every one of these bangles can tell a story of its own. The men in my life, my husbands." She sighs dramatically.

I doodle several entwined circles that form themselves into a shadowy oval, until I hear Alice's voice again.

"Thank you, Clarissa. Mmm … Barbara. Will you tell us a bit about what you want to write, please?"

Barbara smiles in a self-deprecating way that endears her to me instantly. She looks about Rakel's age, but unlike Rakel, who keeps her hair black like Clarissa's, Barbara's hair is a faded white-yellow to match her skin. Her eyes are as green as the sea which I can glimpse behind her.

"I was part of the Black Sash in my youth, and Cassie, my adopted daughter, wants to know more about my life. I'm hoping to be able to write about it, but after all these years, there's a lot I can't recall. I'll try to do my best anyway, for Cassie." She looks down at her fingers with their square, bitten nails.

The woman next to her enters the silence. Her face and neck are burnt a deep brown and her fingers tap on the table like she's practising piano scales.

"Monica, I'm a travel writer." She throws down her sentence like it's a challenge to Alice.

I wonder if she's always this fierce. Or if she's afraid. Maybe she's as anxious in this setting as I am.

"I want to write about the five years I spent in Egypt and the much younger man I was married to for three of those years. I already have a publisher."

There are polite murmurs of congratulations.

Lucy's next. "I'm a mom, and a granny and a great-granny. I've had twelve children and it's for them that I'm writing this. It was their idea – this course was their Christmas present to me."

Lucy beams at us and tells us about the books she's made for each of her children, recording details of their births, their school reports, weddings (one divorce, she whispers), and every good thing that's ever happened to them.

My doodled oval has become a boiled egg with a cracked top. I wonder if I've remembered to place the shop's egg order.

Then it's Rakel's turn. She's brisk.

"I was born in Germany, early in 1938, or possibly late 1937. During the war I was separated from my parents. I don't know anything about my family. I never will, although I've spent years looking for them. I want to write my memoir because I'm beginning to forget my experiences. I want to record my stories for other survivors. Not only of the Holocaust, but of any kind of horror."

She turns to me.

"This is Malak, my chauffeur, and I've forced her to join me in this class."

The others look at my tan skin (by birth, by sun, by machine?) and I see their eyes calculate: Am I really her driver? It's Rakel's attempt at humour, but they don't know that. They don't know that she's trying to give me a succouring foothold. I smile at Barbara and the others, and in my adult voice, the one I reserve for special occasions when I have to deal with strangers, I say, "My sister went missing when I was a teenager. I want to write about that."

I imagine the inaudible releases of breath. They smile back at me. That is, except for Clarissa, who throughout everyone else's brief introductions has been scribbling in her notebook. I am the youngest in this writing class by at least twenty years and the only woman who isn't white. Yes, Amal, that's something I still notice. What can I say, I was born during the apartheid years. I can't stop checking to see if I'm the token person of colour in the room.

Alice gives us a writing prompt, which is to describe a private memory using the words "I remember". She tells us to free-write for ten minutes and she brings out a clockwork egg timer. I remember a story I once read about a woman who'd murdered her unemployed husband and had used some of his ashes in an egg timer after his cremation, so that he finally had a job.

Ten minutes is a lifetime. I add a few flourishes to my egg-doodle while I wait for inspiration, and another memory surfaces: my first driving lesson soon after I'd finished high school and just before my wedding.

I remember the driving instructor knocked on our front door, led me to the car, put me into the driver's seat and got in next to me, expecting me to know what to do simply because I'd been a passenger in a car before. I wanted to explain that I'd travelled in a plane before but no one would have expected me to know how to pilot one.

Now I want to ask Alice how she imagines I can write just

because I've read a book before. But, of course, I don't question Alice. I follow her instructions as I did with the driving-school teacher. Besides, the other women are already moving their pens professionally across the page. So I join them. Or, at least, I pretend to join them by adding a small stream of runny yolk to my doodled egg. Eventually I begin to add words that loiter self-consciously on the edges of my page. They look like children who are wearing new clothes and are afraid of getting themselves dirty.

"Plunge in," says Alice, encouraging us. This is me, plunging.

It's difficult having sex in front of an audience, even if that audience is only one person, and even if that person's a wraith I've conjured into existence, a spectre knitting translucent red-and-purple socks. The click-clack of the four knitting needles gets on my nerves and smothers any hope of passion. And even if I manage to ignore the noisy needles, I can hear her sniffing disapprovingly and then sighing: click-clack, sniff-sniff, click-clack, sigh-sigh, click-clack.

Amal, who else but you would believe that our dead great-grandmother, a woman we never knew when she was alive, often appears to me at the most inconvenient of moments. Like now, while Taj is offering me his routine birthday gift of oral sex. I am trying to enjoy myself, but despite all his technical training and theoretical expertise, he still doesn't get it. He licks at me delicately like I'm chocolate and he's got toothache.

I want this to be over so I can get some sleep before I leave for

Mum's. I'd like to be with her when she wakes up and remembers it's another new year and your birthday today.

I open my eyes and glare at the place where I imagine Oma is sitting, but all I see is the gleaming shadow that is Taj's white doctor's coat, the one his dear Aunty Shireen bought him to congratulate him on his latest qualification. Staring in Oma's direction gives me a painful squint and I close my eyes for a moment.

I wake up as Taj rolls away from me into a snore. I put on the yellowing gown that used to be too big for you, Amal, though it's way too short and tight for me, because you were the size of a fairy. I tiptoe out of the room. Under my feet the wooden floors groan and whisper softly, like well-mannered ghosts. If only Oma were as considerate.

I make my way in the dark to the kitchen and quickly switch on the light to check for bugs. There are only the white counters and no sign of crawling creatures, but I can't get out of the habit of expecting the worst. I've never seen so much as an ant on my kitchen counter, but recently Precious told me that cockroaches can live without their heads for seven days, and now I'm obsessed with the idea of coming across a headless roach. Amal, you must remember Taj's cousin Precious, aka Farid? Of course you can't have forgotten Shireen's one and only child. But what you don't know is that he now lives next door to us and hangs around our house like a spare, unwanted husband.

I fill the coffee machine with water. I can hear Oma telling me: Rooibos tea is better for you, my child.

"Tastes like pee, Oma," I say aloud.

The moment I say that, the moment I accept her comment, I feel Oma's old cat Mrs Truffles rub against me, as warm as if she were alive. I can even hear her purring. I wonder if thirty is too young for senile dementia. What do you think, Amal? Were you ever this age?

After gulping down the coffee and checking my calves for imaginary cat fur, I shower, then get my packed bag from the cupboard. I twist my prematurely greying hair (yes, I've inherited Mum's genes) into my teacher-bun, slide on my driving glasses, and I'm ready. I close the bedroom door on Taj's snores just as the doorbell rings.

It's Precious. I'm only surprised that he came to the front door and didn't climb over the low balcony wall separating our homes as he usually does. Red-eyed, he stands in the dim passageway, swaying gently. Amal, he is still short and skinny, the way they describe coffee these days. When he opens his mouth I can smell he's been celebrating the new year.

"I'm sorry about what happened when we were out yesterday," he says, his eyes downcast.

"Go away."

"But I can—"

"Please go away," I interrupt, and move past him without breathing. Do you remember, Amal, how you taught me to hold my breath whenever we walked past a Christian butchery, so we wouldn't go to hell for inhaling pig fumes?

But before I reach the stairs, I hear him say quietly, almost as though he's speaking to himself, "I miss her too."

I can't deal with Precious today, so I ignore his comment and run down the stairwell into the parking area. Then I'm in the luxury of the doctor's wife's car that Taj bought for my last birthday (which means it's exactly one year and almost a day old). Or maybe I'm confusing the car with the diamond ring he gave me. I'm not good at remembering things from my life.

Soon, I'm on the freeway, which is still busy with New Year's Eve drivers. Most of them are probably drunk. I have this fantasy about being an undercover traffic cop, bearing down on drunk drivers, or those drivers who speed by with toddlers standing on the front seats. But I'm just distracting myself with these silly thoughts. The reality is another new year, another birthday without you, Amal.

The drive to Mum's usually takes about two or three hours, depending on the traffic and my coffee stops. Last night, even though it was my birthday, I didn't go out. I haven't gone out on New Year's Eve since the year of your vanishing. I don't have any friends to invite me out. Apart from Rakel.

Recently, I was rummaging through the Internet and discovered that you and I are Irish twins, as we're born within twelve months of each other. These days that term's considered pejorative, so maybe I should delete it and call us calendar twins.

I wonder how Mum coped with two young children our age. I can't imagine Dad helped out much. She says she was grateful for small things like disposable diapers (she obviously wasn't worried about her carbon footprint back then) and paracetamol. Do you think the medication was for her or for us?

Remember how much we loved being the same age, for one day of every year? Although we hardly looked like sisters, seeing as you were so tiny compared to me. I remember how small and fragile you seemed next to Taj: the two of you looked like one of those couples on the cover of a romance novel, the kind that Bonny reads.

Bonny has been working for us part-time since she started studying to be a teacher two years ago. She's our sales assistant, and she helps us with the baking when we can't cope. She also keeps Rakel company when I take an afternoon off. Not that I do much with my free time. Usually I wander around the streets of our neighbourhood to avoid being alone, window-shopping at the pet store, or browsing through the second-hand bookshop. I only read books by women because, as the writer Grace Paley says: "Women have always done men the favour of reading their work, but men have not returned the favour."

I'm on chatty terms with the shop owner, Maria. I'm probably her best client. Except maybe for Precious, who despite some of his eccentric manners also loves reading. Although our tastes are divergent. Since your leaving I've turned to reading novels about crimes, especially ones with female protagonists, while Precious reads mostly non-fiction. Stuff about bugs and sharks and autobiographies of people no one's ever heard of. I suppose it makes a change for him from his university work (some obscure subject offered by the Religious Studies Department, I always forget what exactly, but it has something to do with feminism and Islam).

Next door to Maria is a laundromat. I often hang out there when I'm waiting for the cupcakes to cool, before I can decorate them. I like watching the clothes through the glass fronts of the washing machines, like sudsy crystal balls. I find it hypnotic. You might think it strange, Amal, but our business is popular and profitable. And since we don't take on more orders than we can handle, my working life is hardly ever stressful. I even do occasional deliveries to Rakel's favourite customers: the primary school across the road, the old-age home two streets away and one or two nearby guesthouses.

When I'm not decorating or baking cupcakes, I spend a lot of time on the Internet. I like to sift through the missing-girl websites. Do you know there are girls missing in every part of the world? The websites describe a case as "open" even when the woman in question has been missing for decades. Individual missing-person websites are the most poignant: Rani, aged 15, brunette, weight approximately 58 kg, missing since 1984. Or Olga, who had a birthday in March and whose mother hoped she'd call that day. Or Jane, who went to the corner store to buy her puppy a new ball and didn't come back to see that puppy grow into a dog. Or Kate, who was last seen at 5 pm walking to her evening university class. And then there's that line on most of the sites: "Help us find our missing loved one, help us find our child." Even when that child is now an adult, or only a bit of bone.

Amal, you'll never guess who introduced me to Internet searches. Mum. Yes, the same woman who refused to use a cellphone when you were around is now a computer expert. She's even set up a website for you. But I've never visited it. What's the point? I know everything about your case.

I don't know how Mum copes after visiting these sites, because they often leave me with a heavy heart. (Actually, I do know how she copes: she quilts.) There are days when I don't want to get out of bed because I keep thinking about all those missing girls and women.

Of course there are Internet tales that give me a boost and make me as high as Precious after a pot-smoking session. I love reading those stories of survival and escape against all odds: girls found, girls rescued, girls reunited with their families after years, after they'd been given up for dead. After their mothers had packed away their clothes and given away their dolls to little girls born long after their vanishings.

Don't imagine for a moment, Amal, that I ever fantasise that will happen to me, to us. I know that you won't be found in a cellar somewhere, blinded from years spent in darkness. I know you won't be in a random car stopped by police at a random roadblock. I know you won't make one last dash for freedom when your captor's back is turned. I don't have any more hopes for a happy ending for any of us.

But let me get back to my latest birthday, which was yesterday. In a moment of loneliness, I let Precious come shopping with me. Maybe it was turning thirty and knowing that somewhere you would be turning thirty-one without me.

So on my shopping trip, Precious wandered around as I tried to find a comfortable bra, without barbed underwire or heavy padding, and, no sooner had I found the perfect one and noticed a buy-two-get-one-free sale on undies, when I caught a glimpse of Precious, his left hand on the marbled thigh of a nearly naked lingerie mannequin. He was sliding the fingers of his right hand up to the wispy-as-smoke panty that barely covered her forever-firm butt. A pair of toddlers had paused in their biscuit mastication to observe him from their vantage point, a parked pram, sleek and silvery, like my car. Their mother, with one hand on the steering mechanism of the buggy, turned around from her hunt in the discount bin in time to see Precious and his nimble fingers approach the panty's secret recesses.

She let out a shriek (the kids' mum, that is, not the mannequin). Security guards materialised like spectres at a séance and frogmarched Precious out, while he twisted and turned to catch a glimpse of me, but I ducked behind a row of pregnant mannequins dressed in maternity clothes. Precious is a big boy, and what with his wealthy stepfather being friends with almost everyone with any political or economic power in this country, I was sure it wouldn't be long before he was out of the security guards' custody. He didn't need my help. But, of course, I couldn't leave without Precious. So I lingered over the rest of my shopping and, fortunately, he joined me as I was paying for my purchases. We drove home in silence and he left the car without saying goodbye to me.

On the road to Mum, a car whizzes by. I glimpse a teenage boy-driver: I'm almost jealous of him and his confidence, his youthful belief in immortality. The last of the car's flashing head-lights vanishes and I'm left in an enveloping darkness which, when I slide down the car's window (only slightly, I'm a woman driving alone) and wave my fingers in the air, feels thick and warm, like honey.

I slip into my most recent dream of you, Amal. Have I men-tioned that I often dream of you? I wonder if you dream about me too. In this dream, the two of us are holding hands, floating together on the Dead Sea.

Malak, you tell me, although we don't actually speak, we use telepathy in dreams, like we did when we were children, *this is like the Great Salt Lake.*

Huh?

In Utah, you say.

Utah. I think of Mormons.

Are they the guys, I ask, *who are entitled to several wives, like Muslim men, or is that another media misconception? I'm sure Mum had a cousin who moved to Utah and became a Mormon.*

The sin of apostasy, you say.

Even now that you're gone, you still have to show how clever you are.

Have you been to Utah? I ask.

Yes. I've been travelling everywhere, since. How about you?

Not really. I went to Amsterdam with Taj, for our honeymoon. I remember, every time I saw something I liked, I kept thinking I'd have to tell you about it. Then I remembered you were missing. The same thing happened when he took me to London. Luckily,

Precious was with us then. He filled the silence the way a child does when his parents have long run out of conversation. And I visited Cousin Zuhra once, on my own.

Up above us, over the dark waters in which we're floating, the sky is the colour of a lilac flower, slowly turning grey. I have a pashmina in that exact shade. Taj bought it in India, a trip that he and Precious went on last year without me, at my insistence. It was one of the times I couldn't get out of bed, except to perform the most basic of tasks.

It looks like rain, I say.

You disagree. You say, *It barely rains here and, besides, we're in a dream, we can stop the rain.*

Nah, let it rain, I say.

And it does, warm fat drops of water, like baby's tears.

You say, *This is how it must have been when we were under Mum's skin.*

There's a long silence and then you say, *It's weird, isn't it? Neither of us will ever know what it's like to be pregnant.*

That sentence bumps into my joy like a car driven by a drunken driver. You see something in my face that makes you tighten your hold on my hand. You say, *Sorry, sorry, remember this is just a dream. Words don't sting in dreams.*

I wake up. My fingers are warm where you've held them.

When I dream about you, Amal, I forget you're gone. But then I wake up and turn around to see Taj in bed next to me, and the memories flood over me.

I sometimes think Taj only became a fertility specialist

because of my predicament. There's nothing wrong with him, you see, Amal. His sperm have a high motility. He's been tested by several specialists and, of course, himself. He even gave up the occasional joint he used to share with Precious the year I told him I wanted a baby. So if it's not him, it has to be me. Yes, I ovulate, but there's a slight hormonal imbalance. They've told me to lose a kilo or two, which I did, and I've tried medication that made me crazy, gave me menopausal symptoms. I don't recommend hot flushes, not even in a Cape winter. It's just one of those things – I can't get pregnant. One of life's little mysteries, like your disappearance, Amal. Taj says conception is difficult even when the people involved are "normal". It's about luck, he says. Good or bad luck, I think, depending on whether or not you want to conceive.

The truth is, sometimes I'm not sure I want a baby. In the beginning, when I was first married, after you went missing, my need for a child was strong, especially on the days I missed you most. I admit I wanted a baby to fill the space left by your disappearance.

It doesn't help that Taj is so understanding. Despite his indiscretions and his selfishness, Taj has been good to me. Not the way he was to you, Amal. He's never looked at me like I was his favourite person in the world. But when I've been sick, he's been there to sponge away my fever and, once, in the middle of the night, when I got my period, he went out and bought me tampons, because I had a silly superstition that if I had them readily available at home, I'd never get pregnant. But after almost eleven years of marriage, it's obvious Taj and I aren't going to have a baby together, any more than you're going to come around to my shop to order three dozen double-fudge cupcakes for your birthday party.

I'm at Mum's turn-off. The smooth tar changes to spitting gravel and there's her house, a white lily set against the sea. In summer, the house, which appears alone in its surrounds, is beautiful in its solitude. In winter, with the wind and rain struggling to get in through the windows, it's the kind of house that makes me long to sleep forever. This is why I can't believe Rakel deliberately seeks winter. Right now she's in Europe for the holidays. She says it's a genetic calling that makes her long for snowy winters every Christmas and warm summers in June. Of course Mum's house isn't really alone, it's only designed to look that way. It's one of a dozen or so homes that are part of a gated community made up of mostly retired people.

I drive up to the house as softly as the car will allow, the same way I duck my head when I'm entering an underground garage on the rare occasions I've driven Taj's double-storey car. Of course Mum won't hear me anyway. Even at this early hour, she'll be awake and out on the front porch, and the crashing waves would have muted the sound of my arrival.

Mum's house is small. It has two bedrooms, one bathroom, and an open-plan kitchen, dining and living room. She's decorated the inside in white, with splashes of red. The walls are white. The tiles are white. She has white blinds on her windows, the block-out kind so that the sun doesn't tan her interiors. It's like Mum's living in a fridge.

I park my car behind her two-door functional vehicle. I imagine her bedroom light is switched on as usual (she's always left a light on in her room, since your disappearance), but I can't see through the protective shades. There are red and white roses planted outside her front door. Snow White and Rose Red. She used to call us that when we were children, after those two sisters living in a tiny cottage with their mother, deep in the forest. Do you remember the tale? A bear (an enchanted prince, naturally) comes along and eventually marries one of the sisters. When Mum told us this story, you always used to say I could marry the bear (as though there was ever any doubt you and the bear-prince were meant to be together). I told you we could share. You smiled at me wisely, and said that wasn't possible. But you were wrong. I am sharing Taj with you, and with the various women he sleeps with. Of course Taj would never have cheated on you, Amal. It's just that I'm not you.

I walk by the front door and around to the side of the house. Mum's sitting in her porch chair, facing the sea, blowing small smoke clouds that waft up to meet their bigger siblings in the sky.

That's right, Mum started smoking after your disappearance. I suppose we all needed to find support in some way after you left, and cigarettes are as good a crutch as any. I think Mum enjoys the ritual of opening a new packet, taking out a cigarette from its foil wrapping, and lighting a match in her cupped palm, more than she does actually smoking them, because I regularly find half-filled packets around her house along with partially smoked cigarettes in white ashtrays.

She doesn't notice me. She's staring out to sea like she needs a guide dog.

I know where she is: she's travelling through the thirty-six hours of labour pains, through the darkness of two nights until you made your appearance at sunrise that first day of the new year, looking around you, Mum always told us, with the clearest and most hopeful of gazes. So they called you Amal. Hope. The same kind of hope which springs eternal in our mother's breast that one day you will walk through the door, smile, and say, "Sorry, I forgot what the time was." The kind of thing you used to say after you'd come home from a late-night snogging session with Taj.

Mum glances away from the sea and offers me the same polite smile I wear around Taj's relatives.

"Happy birthday for yesterday, sweetie. Here's your present." She pats the package on the bench next to her.

"Thanks."

The gift is covered in the green, gold and red of Christmas wrapping-paper. I know what it will be. A variation on what Mum's been giving me every year since I became her only child. A jersey of some sort. She must imagine that wherever you are, you're cold, Amal. I know I do.

I mirror her smile, pick up the gift and clutch it to my stomach. Mum slides up on the bench so that I can sit next to her, but even seated I have to bend low for the exchange of an awkward kiss. As we separate, tendrils of her grey hair hug my black and white curls.

"I've made crumpets." Perhaps she didn't sleep at all last night. She motions towards her kitchen. Mum demonstrates what's left of her love through food.

"They're on the table. There's cream in the fridge. The electric beater's on the blink, so I had to whip it by hand, but I added some lemon juice to thicken it. There's real maple syrup from Sara. Eat them while they're still warm." She shoos me away with her hand towards the house.

Sara's a Canadian woman Mum met on the Internet. Her daughter went missing around the same time you did. She hasn't come back either.

The early sunlight, weak, like milky tea, enters the kitchen through its solitary window. I have a sudden childhood memory of Dad sipping tea out of a chipped brown saucer. When I was little I thought men and cats drank from saucers. I remember my surprise the first time I saw a male neighbour standing in his garden at twilight, watering his lawn with one hand, the other holding a mug from which he would take the occasional sip. Amal, do you remember? You and I were in the garden catching ladybirds. "What's he doing?" I asked you. "Why's he drinking like a woman?" You paused for a long time, and then you said, "Some men are just different."

I spoon chilled cream over the surface of a warm crumpet and watch it sink into the cake. The cream fades with the slightest of traces, leaving a shadowy stickiness, something like what was left behind when you vanished. I take the stopper off the maple syrup, one of those old bottles that I imagine could hold a genie. The syrup is redolent of springtime in a foreign land. I add another tablespoon of cream and slip the crumpet, whole, into my mouth. I eat several more standing up as I listen to the waves greeting the sand. Then I call out to Mum that I'm going for a nap.

At the door to the spare room, my room, I tilt my face away from the wall so that I don't have to look at your remembrance quilt hanging there, Amal. Instead, I climb under the duvet of the double bed, bought especially for me and Taj, although he's never spent a night here, and pull it over my head. The bed with its red duvet and red sheets makes me think of the operating theatres in which Taj earns his living. I'm exhausted, but I can't sleep.

After a while, I force myself to look at your quilt. Shortly after you went missing, Mum took up quilting and yours is the first one she made. She sewed it by hand and, with the eye of a mathematician, drew pieces of satin, silk, cotton and muslin from your life into a story. The first square is the pink of your favourite baby blankie, the one you slept with until you were ten (yes, I noticed). The last is made from the sleeping bag you used on your last camping trip with Dad. In between, Amal, you'll recognise your favourite black leather jacket, the yellow checks of a much-loathed school pinafore, the green of an embarrassing matric dance dress, the gown you wore at your engagement party, and the red ribbon from your Dorothy costume.

The squares are threaded together with white cotton, and the sashing, the interior border between each block, is made from the blank satin of your wedding dress. The quilt glows, and, there, in the main border, Mum has embroidered her tears, disguised to look like blue-green drops of shimmering sea. Mum protects the quilt with an opaque curtain on the bedroom window, one so impenetrable that the room is always heavy with shadow.

I can't sleep here. I'll try Mum's room.

Through the window I can see her surrounded by a foggy halo like she's the patron saint of smokers. I climb into her all-white bed with its cool sheets that smell of Chanel No. 5 and menthol cigarettes.

But still I can't sleep. Maybe it's being in such a feminine bed after years of sharing one with Taj. Lying here now, I remember the night I agreed to marry him.

Matric exams were over. I looked out from the top window of my bedroom and saw Precious in the garden, his shoulders shaking and his head invisible, like a mourning tortoise. The phone rang. I remember Mum crying in her bedroom, holding your never-to-be-worn wedding dress, Amal. Dad weeping in the garage, bent over the bonnet of a 1950s Ford convertible in which he'd hoped to drive you to your wedding reception. I remember Precious answering the phone. It was the hotel to confirm the flower arrangements for your approaching wedding in February. Although you'd been gone for several months, Amal, no one had thought of cancelling the reception.

That night, Taj and Precious, with me in the middle, sat beneath the fig tree where the three of you used to sit most nights, planning your futures, while Precious smoked weed and kept you entertained with his observations on life.

"Do you want to get married?" Taj asked me.

I turned to look at him closely for the first time in weeks. He looked back at me. The skin on his face was ashen, and when his eyes met mine I saw the indigo smudges beneath them, like stagnant pools. I noticed the bones in the hollow of his throat and the outline of ribs under his white T-shirt, which showed every time he inhaled. Perhaps I'd never looked at him properly before. He was just the man you said you loved, Amal, and although I was jealous of the attention you lavished on him, resentful of the time you two spent together alone, he'd never seemed concrete until that moment.

Some part of my brain acknowledged that his proposal was crazy. He must have known that too. But then everything had become insane since your disappearance, Amal, so the idea of marrying Taj seemed almost normal. We both loved you, we were both bereft. Maybe if we were married we'd find the space to grieve for you together, forever, while the rest of the world went on. It seemed so simple. So natural. Your bridal jewellery was made. Your turquoise bridesmaids picked. Your honeymoon paid for and your marriage home bought. The perfect fairytale wedding was waiting for me, even if I was a changeling.

Mum and Dad stopped crying separately to talk together. I

thought I was making them happy. I thought it was the right thing to do. But the week after my wedding, our parents separated for good. Dad said, "I need more children. I'm only forty-four, I'm young for a man." My hands were still jaundiced with bride-henna when they put our childhood home up for sale, when Mum moved away to be closer to your point of vanishing and Dad started dating (his word, indicative of all the American sitcoms he watched). He got himself a new wife, unsullied by sad memories, who seemed to have stepped out of a box with a past as clean and smooth as a sea-washed pebble. You'll never guess who Dad married. Liesbet, that blonde wondergirl you met at varsity. Only four years older than me.

In the first few months of our marriage Taj used to buy me those fat red carnations you loved. Eventually I had to ask him to stop because their smell reminded me of you, of the scent you have in my dreams of you, the ones that stay with me all through the next day, fine threads of you which slowly disintegrate like spider webs between my memory's fingertips. If only I could have one of those dreams now, but these memories are keeping me awake. I give up on my nap and go to find Mum.

She's in the kitchen drinking herbal tea.

"How's Taj?" Dutiful question, tick it off the list.

She hands me a cup and saucer.

"Fine, working."

I try to take the teapot from her but she moves it out of my reach. Pouring tea is another ritual Mum enjoys. I think it's because of Oma's influence. Do you remember Oma reading our teacups when we were little? You were always going to marry a tall dark handsome man and I was going to be your bridesmaid. Just goes to show you can't trust a ghostly fortune teller.

"Your father?"

She cuts a lemon into thin, almost translucent sections.

"Okay. We spoke yesterday."

She opens a square plastic container and offers me an oatmeal biscuit. We sit at the kitchen table, listening to the ocean, sipping tea. I yearn for a cappuccino. And you.

Dad lives close to Celestial Cupcakes, and although I often see him walking by with his children, we rarely visit each other. His wife has had five daughters in the space of as many years, their birthdays all in August. If there's such a thing as Irish quintuplets, she's given birth to them. The youngest bears the strangest resemblance to you, Amal. Maybe some of Mum's DNA had rubbed off on him after all their years together and it finally surfaced in that baby. The older girls look as though their mother had taken a cutting of herself and grown them in a hothouse. Which is possible. She's a university lecturer now, specialising in some kind of botany research, possibly the same thing that you were interested in. Whenever I visit Dad, we never talk. His daughters surround him, they come between us like a hedge of chatty, noisy, laughing, demanding foliage with thorns protecting their father from his previous life, from me. And you, of course.

Mum breaks into my reverie with the news that Sara's invited her to Quebec in the Canadian spring. I wonder why she's bothering to tell me. We both know Mum will never leave her home, not when there's the tiniest hope that you may return.

"I'm going."

I swallow a sliver of lemon with my tea.

"Really?" I reach for a biscuit to chew over this surprise.

Mum's hardly left this house to do grocery shopping since she moved into it soon after my wedding. Maybe now that you've been gone over a decade she's finally prepared to let go.

She says, "I'll visit you later this month, or maybe next month. I'm running low on fabric anyway, so I need to come into town soon. And, of course, I need a new passport and I have to make visa enquiries, although I can probably do that on the Internet." She motions typing with one hand. "There's that cousin of ours somewhere in Canada. I'll look him up. Last I heard he was rehabilitating ex-zoo animals."

"Alcoholic chimpanzees?"

Mum smiles at me. But it's the kind of smile she could use to thicken the fresh cream instead of lemon juice. She continues to discuss Sara and says she's excited about the visit.

I'm used to Mum being so far away you need a Ouija board to reach her. I'm familiar with the single syllables she uses to pass as conversation, or worse, the words of pretend interest, like *really, nice, lovely*. Or just *mmm*. I can't get used to this new Mum. She's making plans for her future. Of course she hasn't said a word about it being your birthday yet. That may be a bad sign. Or a good sign. As you can tell, I'm not always good at interpreting signs.

Mum gets up from the table and says she'll make us a tomato and mozzarella salad for lunch. She begins to dribble olive oil into a bowl, adds some coarse salt and asks me to get basil leaves from her herb patch out on the patio.

To me the herbs all look the same, like weeds. I have to sniff at several pots before I can distinguish basil from the others. Even so, I nibble at a leaf just to make certain. You and Mum often cooked together. I would hear your giggling even when I was deeply submerged in the voices of my novels, high up in my reading room in the attic. I hate cooking, which must sound strange seeing I have a career in baking, but I only got involved in Celestial Cupcakes because of Rakel.

After we were married, Taj and I moved into the townhouse he'd chosen as a surprise wedding gift for you, close to the hospital where he still works. It was supposed to be a starter home, a temporary residence before the first baby arrived, before we moved into the sort of home Shireen would choose. You know what I mean, Amal, a house complete with indoor swimming pool, tennis court, a garden needing endless maintenance, and stuffed with useless ornaments needing constant dusting. A mini-version of Shireen's house, in other words.

Even now, eleven years later, when it's obvious to anyone who barely knows us that neither Taj nor I want to move (it took me twenty-seven months to unpack my books), Shireen will call to tell him about a house she's found in some over-priced suburb.

She doesn't feel that a townhouse is suitable for her beloved nephew, The Doctor, and certainly not for a specialist of his calibre. Her words.

We live in a complex of nine townhouses, built in pockets of three. We're in the middle of our particular group. If you face the mountain, which our balcony does, Precious is on the left (like the angel who records your bad deeds) and Rakel is on our right. (Amal, it's entirely your fault that I still imagine the right shoulder's angel in a white dress and a golden halo and the left shoulder's angel with horns and a tail.)

All the houses are built along similar lines: an en-suite main bedroom, one guest room and bathroom – not that we ever have guests, except for an occasional visit from Mum, so I keep my books in there – and there's also a small living room and a separate kitchen. We have a study too, but that belongs to Taj, and it's an unspoken rule that I'm not allowed inside it. Our house is sparse and functional. Our only wall decoration was put up by Mum: an Ayatul Kursi in silver with a black frame, Mum's way of reminding us of Allah's power over the cosmos.

Unlike mine, Rakel's home is cluttered and this is why I love it. Her living-room walls and furniture are covered with photos of people who look as though they could be related to her. But they're not. They're just photos of strangers she finds in antique stores on her trips abroad. She says they make her feel like she's part of a huge extended family. Amal, I'd rather have those photos as my relatives than the vast family I married into.

When we moved in, Rakel was already a resident. A few

months later, the man next door died and Precious moved in without our knowledge or his mother's. Oh, the drama. Shireen wept and wailed. Her one and only son was leaving her home and he wasn't even married. But Precious was steadfast. Nothing would move him, not even Shireen's daily deathbed scenes. Not even the 2 am calls from her to Taj (Precious refused to answer his phone), asking Taj to climb over the balcony and awaken her son so he could rescue her, because black men (always black men) wearing ski masks were attempting to murder her. Eventually Uncle Santa managed to calm her down (I'm sure he feeds her tranquillisers on the sly), and after a few months she relented. Sometimes I think Shireen would have preferred that Taj The Doctor was her real son and not Precious.

The one thing I like about living in this townhouse is that we don't have space to entertain Precious and Taj's family members. On the rare occasion we do have guests, they're usually Taj's colleagues, and even then we often take them to restaurants. And they're very civilised. They don't lean over and ask me how much I paid for the rug in the living room, or the bathroom tiles, and where I bought the flatscreen TV, and if I know that I can get the electricity fixed so we need never pay for the service.

I hardly see anything at all of Mum and Dad's relatives. They seem to prefer thinking that I've vanished along with you, Amal, like we've both been struck by the same disease. If I hadn't met Rakel, I'm not sure what would have happened to me. Maybe those relatives would have been proved right. Maybe I'd have become mislaid like you.

Rakel lured me into her life with the scent of vanilla. When I first got a whiff of her cupcakes, drifting from the open balcony, I thought Precious was burning a new kind of incense to camouflage his dagga-smoking. I've grown to hate incense. They burnt dozens, hundreds of incense sticks in those first few weeks after you'd gone. But when I went out onto the balcony, I saw the trays of cupcakes cooling on her table. She came out. She said something about how they weren't ready but would I like to taste one. She used my name when we spoke – I realised we must have met before, but I couldn't remember. I ate three, straight from the tray. She said she'd always wanted to own a bakery, that after she'd started baking cupcakes all her friends had encouraged her to open up her own business. I told her I couldn't bake and, even if I wanted to, my oven was broken.

But, later, when Rakel needed another oven, because her business was expanding, she got me involved. And that's how I finally unpacked the dusty, unopened wedding gifts and found food processors and measuring cups and kitchen scales. The kinds of gifts given to traditional brides as opposed to the fraudulent one I was. Rakel made baking look less like tedium and more like alchemy as I learnt to transform snowy flour, luminous eggs and grains of honey-coloured sugar into enchanting sensations that tasted and smelt like childhood, that made me hear your laughter on those nights before Eid when we'd raid the kitchen together, while Mum turned a blind eye.

That first day, while I ate her cupcakes, Rakel asked me how I was enjoying my studies. I didn't tell her that I spent most of my lectures sketching pencil-crayon kites in my notebooks, with pink billowing tails and red bows. Sometimes, when I was feeling adventurous, I drew colourful balloons instead, with long swirling pieces of string waving in a dark sky. Nonetheless, I passed my exams that year, a combination of my ability to reiterate the lecturer's words, Rakel's cupcakes and the warmth she brought to my life. I hadn't realised how lonely I was until we became friends. Even though I had a husband, I saw very little of Taj, and when he was around, he made few husbandly demands. He was always working, or studying, or travelling, or going out to places he never told me about. And, of course, I was too polite to ask. So I was free to experience university life, to make friends, to party. Not that I did anything more exciting than read in the university library.

In my last year of studies, Rakel and I found our store. She was the one who noticed the "To Let" sign in the small shop's dusty window. She invited me to be her partner.

Mum lent me my half for the business from the money she'd inherited from Oma, and Celestial Cupcakes was born. Within a year, I'd repaid Mum. I'm sure you'll find it hard to believe, Amal, that your little sister is involved in a baking business. I know our mother still finds it hard to fathom.

Now I go back inside to Mum with more basil than we need and she says not to worry, she'll freeze it. I'm feeling tired again and, after lunch, I am finally able to nap for a while, this time in my room. I try to ignore the Silent Wailing Wall of Amal.

I'll bet you're surprised about Mum's quilting hobby. At the end of her first year living in this complex, Mum met a woman, Wendy, who had come to finish writing a book of poems. Wendy taught Mum a few quilting stitches and helped her to begin your quilt. After she left, with her book of poems complete, Mum continued her studies, courtesy of the Internet.

Mum's quilts take forever to make. She sews them all by hand. It's kind of hypnotic watching Mum at work. The repetitive motion of needle in and needle out has a rhythm that always manages to calm me. And watching her usually puts me to sleep. In fact, just thinking about watching her is making me sleepy.

I doze briefly and wake up when Mum comes into the bedroom.

"Did you have a nice nap?"

I nod, and smile at her.

"I'm going to work on my latest quilt." She waves her hand behind her in a gesture that indicates the bench and table outside where she usually works in good weather. It also serves as her lookout point. I often imagine Mum thinks that one day you'll wash ashore, as a broken seashell.

"Would you like to join me?" Mum asks. She's making an effort, so I agree, and go out into the summer day. I wonder how Rakel is enjoying her much colder holiday. We close the shop from Christmas Eve until the schools reopen in January. Rakel travels to Europe, but I usually spend my time at home reading, or visiting Mum. Taj works through December so that his colleagues who celebrate Christmas can have some time off (he's thoughtful that way). So I understand when he always claims to have to work on your birthday, Amal. It may be his way of coping with the grief of your absence.

It's good to be off work for a while, not that my job can be described as stressful. In fact, Dad says I'm semiretired like him. Since his heart surgery, his hours have been flexible too. Did I mention Dad's had a bypass operation? Maybe that's what having five daughters in rapid succession will do to a man. Although, of course, Dad has seven daughters, including you: one for every level in Muslim heaven.

After his surgery, Dad acquired a manager at his business, one he insists can't be trusted. Yes, Dad still sells second-hand cars. If he reads this he'll be furious at my description. So perhaps I should write that Dad still sells investments: luxury vintage vehicles. The kinds of cars that should come with their own au pair, because they're as high maintenance as Shireen after her second (or third?) foray into cosmetic surgery. Which we're not supposed to mention. Whenever she has something done that makes her look like a younger more plastic version of herself and people ask why she looks different, she tells them she's had a new hairdo.

Outside, I pause to look at the sea. I don't always notice the beauty of my surroundings and I often take them for granted, like a man married to a lovely woman who stops appreciating her looks after the exchange of rings. But pretty as the sea is, I find it disturbing, especially at night when you can hear it roaring like a beast in pain. I don't actually like it during the day either, too many people around, especially in summer.

This sea is close to where you went missing, Amal. So it is the place where Mum moved to almost immediately after my wedding. I think she was glad when I got married. It freed her for you, Amal. She could concentrate on your absence without having to worry about me. I don't think she really minded Dad's departure either. We were distractions.

The quilt that Mum's working on now is another sad one, one of her memory quilts. This one has been commissioned by a friend of one of her neighbours, whose secretly pregnant daughter was drowned by her wealthy, married lover. Mum's become adept at making these memory quilts. She gets to know the subject of her quilt by meeting with the person's family and friends over several weeks. She pores over photos and videos, whatever they can provide, as a way of getting inside the head of the missing person before she begins the actual quilt. Her current project has been six months in the making, and it's probably going to be several more months before Mum sews the final exquisite stitch with her flashing thimble and tapered fingers, before she stitches the top cloth to the batting and, in turn, to the back of the quilt. She's making it with lots of golds and russets and greens, the dead daughter's favourite colours.

It was Cousin Zuhra who turned Mum's creative therapy into a career, who forced her to begin a quilting cottage industry.

These days Zuhra's a lecturer in feminist fairytale studies at a university in Florida. Zuhra got Mum to create her a quilt based on the re-imagined fairytales she's been writing for her blog.

Mum's fairytale quilt looks as though it is lit from the inside. It shows a frog being swallowed, at the princess's urging, by her spoilt cat, there's Sleeping Beauty poisoning her narcissistic prince, there's Cinderella running off towards a library rather than a dubious happily-ever-after, and various other figures from Zuhra's tales. Zuhra's friends and colleagues loved it, and the quilt soon found a semi-permanent home in an art gallery. Zuhra said she had to have Mum's work framed behind glass to prevent it from being damaged by all the touches it kept inviting. When Zuhra insisted on getting her quilt back from the gallery, the owner commissioned a series of similar quilts. Mum had to employ three women from town to help her, and all their pieces were immediately sold out. There's a long waiting list for Mum's fairytale work. Mum designs the quilt and gets the others to sew the individual squares, but it's her job to put the pieces together into the final quilt, and she makes a small fortune selling these pieces of art.

Zuhra's working on arranging an exhibition of all Mum's work soon. I don't think Mum's all that keen on the idea, especially as she feels she isn't solely responsible for all the work, at least not the fairytale ones. Zuhra wants the quilt exhibition to travel the world. I never imagined that Mum would agree to that, but now that she's contemplating a Canadian trip, maybe she'll consider it.

I watch Mum moving her thimble (gold today to match the fabric) to her middle finger, pressing that finger hard against the needle's eye, making elaborate glinting stitches. She says it's a rocking stitch, and because this quilt is not going to be decorative like most of her others, she is using a thread that's thicker, stronger and longer wearing. Her needle has a short, thin shaft, which she pushes with ease through the layers of her fabric sandwich, making something nourishing out of a dead woman, to fill the hole in a desolate mother's heart. I notice she's using a wooden frame today; she wants the tension on this quilt to be perfect, no shifting of the layers. Her fingers are moving constantly towards herself, following the light markings made with the soap slivers she prefers. I try to ignore Mum's rhythmic fingers and immerse myself in my mystery novel. But I can't focus. The sea's too noisy.

Mum looks up from her sewing, then puts down the quilt. She says, "Did I ever tell you Amal was born with a caul covering her face?"

Taj has told me about this rare event when a baby is born with part of the amniotic sac covering its face. He says it's considered a good omen, but I've never heard of it happening to anyone I know.

"The nurse told me that I could get a lot of money for it if I sold it to a sailor. But I told her it belonged to the child. I remember Oma telling me that children born with the caul could see ghosts."

Could you see ghosts, Amal? I think it was only Oma you

could see, right? But then why could I see her as well? Maybe it was because of your presence. You always had a way of making me see things clearly.

"If Oma hadn't died just before Amal was born, she would have made a drink out of the caul and fed it to her, to protect her from the bad spirits and make her lucky. I didn't really believe in those kinds of superstitions, but I made your father bury it along with the afterbirth anyway. Later, I regretted that I hadn't followed the rules. Maybe if I had …

"Amal did seem to suffer from night terrors more than other children, certainly more than you, and she was always having conversations with invisible friends, but then so were you. So maybe it was a normal stage of development. It stopped when she went to school and started to learn the alphabet. Do you remember she taught you to write and to read too? She was so clever. It's because of her you were reading and writing before you ever got to school."

Mum looks down at her hands. She begins to pick at a hangnail.

"I remember the day after she was born, in that same hospital where Taj works. Did I ever tell you that? I know you'll tell me it's a coincidence. After the birth my milk came in immediately. Rivers of milk. There was too much for one baby. A nurse took the excess away for the white mothers in the bottom ward. The nurse said she wouldn't tell the mothers where the milk had come from. I suppose she meant *who*. I guess those white mommies would have found it offensive to have their babies fed on my milk. I was resentful. All that time spent pumping milk, only to have it given away to someone else's baby. These days they freeze breast milk, maybe they didn't do it then, I don't know."

That's the only time she speaks of you, Amal, although I spend two nights with her.

Things (Not) to Do in a Broken Lift

Our pens or pencils poised like dutiful schoolgirls, we are seated at Alice's wooden table, each with a steaming cappuccino, which we sip from time to time to avoid talking to our classmates. Or maybe that's just me.

From Alice's window I have the view of a rippled sea, and I wonder if Mum is at her lookout point too.

"When you write a memoir, you don't simply record your life story from the past to the present," says Alice. "You write about things that touched you, and you write with the benefit of hindsight. Last time we met, I gave you an 'I remember' writing assignment. Is there anyone who would like to read from their work?"

"I would," says Rakel. "I'm probably the oldest here and sometimes I forget important events, but this is my earliest memory."

It was my birthday. I remember my mother letting me help her light the candles, but I can't recall how many there were, or if my father was there. I had a new doll with gold hair and a white dress identical to the one I was wearing. Kay, my nanny, had sewn both our dresses. The doll was napping in my arms while I drowsed in my mother's. Mother was asleep. I was sure of this. She couldn't have been faking because even when I poked her big tummy with one small finger she didn't budge. But the lamp on her side of the bed showed me how her hilly stomach moved. I think the baby inside of her was trying to touch me through my mother's skin. I put my finger directly on her flesh, into the open space made by the button that had come undone. My mother's skin smelt only of my mother. I didn't like to think of the baby living deep inside her, but she said I should not be frightened of it, that soon a darling creature would come out of her, and it would look like me, and I'd love it the way I loved her and Kay and my father.

Kay came into my mother's room. Is this the same evening? I'm not sure. The room was lighter, so it could have been daytime. Kay didn't knock. Kay always knocked on my mother's door, a light tap-tapping. Then she would wait until she was told to come in. But that day Kay didn't knock. She came straight in and shook my mother awake. Her hands were fluttering and her knuckles were blue. I remember thinking her hands must have been cold. Kay spoke in a whisper that became a scream. She grabbed me, and her hands were not cold after all: her palms were hot and sticky on the skin of my thighs as she settled me against her waist.

I reached down to my mother's bed to grab my doll, but all I got was one soft black shoe. I remember that Kay and I took the doll to the same shoemaker that made my shoes. He fashioned hers from bits of the leather left over from mine. I still have that doll shoe, a *tiny black leather ballet slipper, which in seven decades has never fallen to pieces, although once it became green around the edges when I forgot it near the back of a mildewed closet.*

I never smelt my mother's skin again. I searched for her for several years in bottles of perfume. Decades later, when I was in Ontario, cherry-picking with my second husband, I found my mother, the strange perfume of her skin, on the breeze. I still can't eat cherries today. I believe it would be a kind of matricide.

Rakel has never told me this story before and my first reaction is to feel jealous, because she's shared it with these other women. I know her facts. Born Jewish in France during the war, spirited away by her governess when her parents were imprisoned, going from one safe house to another, even living with monks for a while, until she found herself post-World War Two in a starving England, adopted by a woman living on her own who'd been yearning for a child after the death of her infant son. I know about her fruitless search for her parents. I know about her three marriages. Her love affairs. Her travels. Now I know her first memory.

Celestial Cupcakes is blissfully air-conditioned, but even so I find myself uncomfortably hot. It's February, the traditional month of Chocolate-Love-Consumerism. I smile professionally at the customer's request and try not to look judgemental. It's not that I care, really, it's just that I have a sensitive stomach. Later, when I'm telling Rakel about the customer's order, she shrugs and reminds me that I'm the one who came up with the range of breast-shaped cupcakes, after all, so I shouldn't be squeamish about this customer's request. I don't see how she can compare the two: mine were made to highlight Breast Cancer Awareness Month. Every breast-shaped cupcake we sold got you a little pink ribbon. It's not like I'm a food pornographer.

"Coprophilia isn't that unusual," says Rakel.

"There's a word for it?"

"There's a word for everything, my dear."

I don't agree. What's the word for marrying your missing sister's fiancé to stop your mother going mad?

Amal, do you remember the last Valentine's Day you and Taj shared? He sent so many flowers to the house that Mum said every breath she took was carnation-scented.

Rakel sails off to have a conversation with Bonny about a failed batch of blueberry icing and I'm left with the task of fashioning a Valentine's cupcake out of chocolate to look like excrement. It seems like a cruel and unusual punishment.

Earlier today, Dad came by for a cupcake and a brief visit, which was an unexpected occurrence. Mostly he doesn't visit, except on the odd occasion when he comes in with Liesbet. Maybe she's forbidden him private visits. But sometimes I wonder if Dad hasn't prohibited himself from seeing me because I'm a reminder to him that you're gone.

He looked tired. I reminded him, spitefully, that at fifty-five, or thereabouts, he's young for a man. He looked at me in surprise. He's begun to colour his thinning hair, but I don't think he's realised that his eyebrows need touching up too. I don't know why he bothers. I wouldn't at his age. Mum's hair is white and she looks good. But maybe he wants to look younger so that when you come back he'll still be familiar to you.

I see Dad performing his mother-duck act most Saturday mornings when they all walk by the shop on their way to do chores. There must be plenty of chores to perform with a family that size. Liesbet always brings up the rear to make sure none of her offspring gets lost.

"How are you, Malak?" she'll ask, and peer deeply into my eyes, her head cocked to one side like she really cares about my answer. Maybe she does. After I've muttered something and she's nodded understandingly, she'll buy each of the girls a cupcake, insisting on paying for them, even though I never offer them for free. She doesn't get any for herself or for my father. She'll pat his round belly and say, "Nothing for you or me today, dearest." But he'll lick a bit of topping from one or two or all five of his daughters' choices while his wife is distracted. Actually, Amal, I like watching Liesbet and her daughters together. I like watching her wiping smudged icing off a dewy cheek, or helping a plump hand hold a daisy cupcake, or even watching the littlest one dither between choosing green or blue icing as her topping.

They're all spoilt for choice in our store. There are so many options, from plain vanilla (made with real vanilla direct from the orchid, none of that vanilla-flavoured stuff) with buttery icing and hundreds and thousands, to tiny wedding cupcakes, three tiers high, with miniature marzipan bridal couples on top. In spring we have daisy cupcakes with sugar butterflies hovering above them, and in summer there are fresh fruit cupcakes with tiny edible umbrellas. Winter cupcakes have silvery icicles and little snowmen, which are always popular when there's snow on the mountain. We're renowned for our kiddies' birthday cupcakes; anything from tarantulas to hamburgers. There are also the inevitable baby shower cupcakes and Halloween cupcakes, the most popular of which are those with marshmallow skeletons. Mother's Day cupcakes are pink blossoms on fresh vanilla cream while Valentine's Day's include hearts in all sizes and those of the less sweet, more sexy variety, from frilly undies to body parts (don't judge me, Amal, I have to follow the demands of the buying public).

The most clichéd cupcake I've ever made was a "Will you marry me?" cupcake with a diamond ring shoved into the centre (after baking). I didn't encourage the client and I was proved right when the bride-to-be swallowed the whole thing, ring and all, and had to have an enema. This reminds me, we also have vegetable cupcakes. Broccoli, for some reason, is the most popular.

My favourite are the book cupcakes. They come in any flavour but all have a fondant book on the top with an exact copy of the book's cover made in rice print. These cupcakes are popular with book clubs.

But the cupcakes we're most famous for, the ones for which we're renowned throughout the cupcake world, are our guardian angel cupcakes. We make chocolate, strawberry and vanilla angels, all with silver-coloured sugar wings and spun-sugar halos. Did you know there's a guardian angel for every day of the week? I wonder what happened to the guardian angel on the day you disappeared. I suppose even angels have to rest sometimes.

Thanks to Rakel and Bonny and Kwezi, our other assistant, who takes orders, does displays and is our best salesperson, I am able to spend most of my time in the kitchen, out of sight, baking and beautifying the cupcakes.

Decorating gives me lots of time to daydream or to consider my night-time dreams. I never dreamt of you until after my marriage, Amal. In the first dream, at least the first dream that I remember, you were practising a magician's act, suspended upside down in a vertical glass coffin filled with water. Your hands and feet were manacled. You twisted and turned, but we both knew there was no escape. You were dying before my eyes. I remember waking up, slick with sweat and reaching for Taj, but he wasn't there.

I often dream of you in or around water. I know this is weird because I remember that you hated water. You were like a fussy cat around it. Remember those weekly swimming lessons Mum insisted on taking us to? You used to refuse to get in the water. You'd stand at the side of the pool, glaring at me as I progressed from doggy to froggy. You said you didn't like the way the water would shoot up your nose and give you a brain-pain like what happened to me when I ate ice-cream. You said that doing the breaststroke was like going nowhere very slowly. Swimming was the only thing I excelled in over you. But in my dreams you don't seem to mind water anymore.

February is one of our busiest months, made all the more hectic because it follows back-to-school parties and, before that, the endless round of December celebrations. This February seems hotter than normal. We're up to our ears in orders, the usual heart-shaped cupcakes, cabbage rose cupcakes, mini-cupcakes made to look like dozens of chocolates in boxes and tiny teddy-bear cupcakes. Sometimes I loathe cupcakes. But this February is also the month my life changes forever.

The momentous day starts in the usual humdrum way. The night before, Taj had been out all night at the hospital bedside of a woman threatening to miscarry. At least, that's what he told me. Without him tossing and turning in bed, I slept more deeply and later than usual. Normally he penetrates my dreams when he gets up before dawn to go to the gym.

I wake up late. The walk to work takes only four minutes, my shower takes three and, as I've given up blow-drying my hair or putting anything other than sunblock and lipstick on my face, I am usually at work by five thirty. I feel grumpy, and it doesn't help that my coffee machine starts leaking instead of heating the water. At work we keep a percolator for ourselves and the clients we're fond of, like Mrs Thomas, a pensioner, who lives on her own with an aged dog. She comes every day around lunchtime and Rakel always offers her a cupcake on the house, with some excuse like: It's a new recipe what do you think? Or: This one didn't bake through properly. Or: Malak didn't do the best job icing this one and would you do us the favour of eating it? She always accepts graciously, and sits there nibbling at the cupcake, sipping at her coffee and gently talking to her dog through the window while he waits for her in a shady spot on the pavement.

So although I can get my caffeine fix at work, what I'll really miss this morning is my routine of drinking coffee on the balcony, which is one of my favourite moments of the day. At that time of the morning, I feel like I'm the only person in the world. Sometimes, on a warm day when the wind is wafting in the right direction, I get a breath of sea air and see its colour mirrored in the light of the sky above my head. And that is when I think of you, Amal.

My day does not get better. My favourite oven, the older of the two we use, stops heating itself without any kind of warning. I get a finger nipped by the whisk of an electric mixer. The milk is sour. Eventually, tired of listening to my swearing, Rakel politely asks me to go off on a delivery to one of her clients, who owns a boutique hotel near our shop.

The hotel has several permanent residents and is run by a woman who insists everyone calls her Madame. She's not French but seems to fancy she is because she's married to a Frenchman, a bald, elderly person, who is seldom more than two steps away from her side.

For some reason best known to Madame, the kitchen is on the third floor of the hotel. When I deliver the two dozen cupcakes for their Sunday tea, I usually use the stairs for some exercise, but in today's heat the lift is irresistible. I carry in the two huge rectangular cardboard trays, one on top of the other, and walk into the lift on my bare feet because I've forgotten my sandals in the car. I always feel better with my toes curled around the accelerator, and Precious says it's an urban myth that driving barefoot is illegal.

As the lift doors, decorated with gold leaf (Madame's Marseilles fantasy), begin to close, a long, thick-fingered hand with blue-green dirt under its nails sneaks inside, keeping them open. A man steps into the lift, and I smell something that reminds me of salad dressing and putty and the sea.

"Hello," he says, nodding at me.

I return the nod, and look down at the cupcakes swimming below me. After a moment, they stop swirling and I can see that they're normal chocolate cupcakes with chocolate mousse piped onto their tops and sprinkled with edible gold dust.

I glance over at him. His hair is short and the colour of Mum's maple syrup. I watch his fingers hover in the air before pressing number five. I've never been beyond the third floor. I notice his grimy nails again. Taj says men with dirty fingernails can give a woman cystitis. Always wash your hands before and after sex. Obviously Taj follows his own instructions because he's never given me any diseases.

This man's smell is making my head sore. But in a pleasurable way. Like the pins and needles you feel when your leg wakes up after it's been caught napping.

He notices me looking at him and smiles down at me. The skin on his cheeks catches the light, shiny like cupcake batter when you've added one egg too many. His smile stretches to his eyes, coffee beans before they're ground, with matching eyebrows. My gaze travels down over a t-shirt and jeans stained with something red, to a pair of flip-flops, then up again to his face. I stare. He reciprocates. The lift pings open.

I swallow, take a deep breath and walk out as the doors begin to close on me. He reaches out a dirty-fingered hands to hold it open.

As I'm nearing the kitchen door, I look back. He is still standing with one hand holding open the door, watching me. I turn back to face the front just in time to stop myself from smashing into the white-and-gold swing doors of the kitchen.

Madame is on the phone. She smiles at me without displacing the smooth, tight skin around her mouth or eyes and motions for me to leave the cupcakes on one of the few empty surfaces in the kitchen. She continues to speak on the phone in a voice too low for me to hear, and hands me an envelope with the cash for the order. I'm dismissed.

I'm contemplating whether to use the stairs when the doors of the lift open and the man with the dirty fingernails begins to step out of it. We collide. His hand reaches out to still my body and his thumb touches the bare skin between the waist band of my pants and my t-shirt. The rest of those fingers and their dirty fingernails splay downward over the thin elastene-cotton combination of my pants. My nose is brought into closer contact with the fine stubble on his skin, which I hadn't noticed before.

"Sorry, wrong floor," he says, reversing into the lift, but not letting go of me, so that I'm pulled deeper into his embrace. I am the first to draw away, but his hands seem to have difficulty letting go of me, like I'm half-chewed bubblegum, sticking and stretching under his fingertips. I search the lift panel for the ground floor button and feel the hair on the back of my neck rising like it does when Mrs Truffles and Oma visit.

Now, Amal, I'm afraid I have to dabble in fiction. I'd like to tell you the words we used in that, our first, conversation. But I can't remember exactly what was said – not the way I can remember the smells and the feelings, the sighing and moaning of the lift as it broke down and became unnaturally silent. But here's what I think happened.

We've almost reached the ground floor when the usually obedient lift squeals, piglet-to-the-slaughter fashion, shudders and jolts, and I find myself losing my footing and falling backwards into his arms. (I know this sounds absurd, predictable. Alice will tell me to do a rewrite.) We're in darkness, but the lift continues to free fall. I'm reminded of an amusement-park ride Precious once tricked me onto. It was a berserk lift in the setting of a 1930s hotel. The lift travelled up and down as well as sideways in a random manner before suddenly dropping dozens of floors. Precious insisted I'd enjoy the ride and said he'd go with me, but moments before it began he slipped away and left me to endure the entire trip in solitary terror.

I feel the stranger's fingers with those dirty fingernails cupping my upper arms as the lift stops, then shudders.

"You okay?" he asks.

I nod.

"Are you okay?" he asks again.

Why is he repeating himself? I wonder. But, of course, he can't see my head nodding in the dark.

"Mmm," I say, my tongue thick as a piece of uncooked steak. "Must be a power outage."

I move away from him, trying to find the wall furthest from him, my outstretched hands searching for something solid, but my big toe makes the connection first. I can't stifle my "ouch!"

"What?"

"It's nothing. I stubbed a toe."

I slide down against the wall and sit tailor-fashion on the cool tiles to nurse my throbbing toe. I try not to think of what Taj would say about the various organisms breeding on the floor.

The lift sways. I hear the teeth of a zipper, the whisper of some movement, then there's light in the form of a small torch. It's the kind of torch, Amal, we used as children when we read under the blankets at night after Dad had turned off the lights.

His beam finds me on the floor and he crouches down across from me, keeping the torch between his knees as he rummages in a backpack I hadn't noticed before. He comes up with a tube of something, smears a bit of it on his fingers, and points the torch at my feet.

"Which toe?"

"Huh?"

"Which toe did you stub?"

I wiggle my foot and its pulsating toe. Even monosyllables have deserted me. He takes my foot in his hand, cups the heel and begins to rub something soft and sticky onto my toe.

"Arnica gel," he answers my unasked question. "It's very useful, even relieves mosquito bites."

I'm reminded of an article I read recently about the "Cinderella procedure", a type of foot surgery that women are using to make their feet narrower.

"Am I hurting you?"

"No."

"There, that should feel better soon."

He taps my toe with his finger twice and then rubs off the excess cream on the knee of his jeans. He puts out the same hand.

"I'm Darya."

"Malak." It's as if I'm saying my name for the first time. It feels like there are cobwebs in my throat, entangling my words. I reach out to take his hand. His fingers are hot, but then so are mine. Our palms stick together for a moment.

"Malak, as in 'angel'?"

"Yes."

"That's a good name, kind of old-fashioned. Were you named after an older relative?"

"No." Please lift the spell, language-witches.

"Who chose it? Your mother?"

I shake my head no, and the ray of his little torch flutters. He jiggles it and the light returns, dimly. I can smell him, but he's become shadowy. Amal, I don't think this is a story I've ever told anyone, not even Rakel, certainly not Taj. Now I find myself telling a shadow-stranger in a broken lift that our parents chose your name with care. That you personified their young love, so they called you Amal, to express their joy. I, on the other hand, was a surprise, making myself felt mere weeks after the birth of their true-love baby. When they needed to choose my name, immediately after your first birthday party, they discovered that during the celebrations you had thrown the book of names that had been in our father's family for three generations into the toilet, presumably to drown. (Yes, Amal, I know you'll say this was not a case of sibling malevolence, but I wonder. You always were a bit selfish.) Dad was able to rescue one page, and the only visible name on it was Malak.

He doesn't interrupt. When I'm done I feel exhausted, like I've been walking uphill. I don't tell him the other story, the one Oma told us. Do you remember it, Amal? She said she'd tried to blow the name of her choice into our parents' ears at your birth, but they couldn't have heard her clearly. Oma always wanted a little girl called Almas, meaning diamond. She made us promise that when we had daughters we'd call one of them Almas.

Darya's torch vibrates delicately and we return to the shadows.

He says, "This is weird. It's like being dead with your eyes open. No wonder we pray for nur in the graves of the dead."

"Unless, of course, you didn't particularly like Nur, then you wouldn't want her in your grave."

"What?" he asks.

He thinks I'm nuts.

"Ah, well, Nur's a girl's name, isn't it? Or maybe it's androgynous. Like yours. Your name sounds feminine with that vowel at the end."

"Right. I'm named after a river. My father's suggestion, although my parents spoke different languages. It could be something was lost in the translation."

He's moved his attentions to my other foot, and now both my soles are alight. I'm afraid of moving them, in case he stops.

"Someone should rescue us soon," he says.

His words fill me with disappointment.

"You don't have any of those cupcakes on you somewhere?" he asks.

"No."

"You make them?"

"I have a shop close by. Well, I'm in partnership with someone, and we own a cupcake shop. Celestial Cupcakes."

"I've seen it," he says, sounding surprised. "I've walked past it once or twice. The name's cute. You named it after yourself?"

"Not exactly. My partner Rakel chose it. Angel cupcakes are our speciality."

"That's charming. I like it."

I'm absurdly pleased, delighted that he likes our obvious, frivolous name. I feel like a bowl of over-whipped fresh cream turning to soft butter. Is this how a twelve-year-old girl in the throes of her first crush feels?

"So how long are you staying in Cape Town?" I ask in an attempt to exorcise the adolescent in my head.

"I live in Cape Town."

He lives here! twelve-year-old shrieks with delight in my brain.

"This guesthouse stay is supposed to be for a week or two, while the builders are destroying my home studio under the pretext of renovating it."

I'm glad he decided to revamp his home. And to move into this particular place, so I could meet him.

"So, your dad chose your name," I say. "How come he wanted to name you after a river?"

"I'm not sure. I never got to ask him. We never met."

"Oh." There's a silence between us until curiosity gets the better of me and I ask him why they never met.

"It's a long story. But since no one appears to be rescuing us, I'll tell you. Wait, I may not have cupcakes, but I've got some water. And a chocolate bar. Here." His fingers find mine and he places a small bottle of water into my hand. I open it and take a sip, then another. I didn't realise how thirsty I was until I begin to drink.

"My mom's South African, but my father was an Iraqi, a Christian one. Most people I tell are surprised that there's a religion outside of Islam in Iraq."

I pretend I'm not most people.

"They met in England. She was visiting relatives. He'd come

over years before to study engineering, but had stayed to teach Arabic at the local university. Although he was often home-sick, his father, my grandfather, insisted he stay in England where he believed my dad had a chance at a better life."

He reaches for the water bottle. His fingers linger on mine.

"When my grandmother died, my grandfather didn't let my father know about her death until she was long buried, so that my father wouldn't go home for the funeral and interrupt his studies. My grandfather believed in the 'cruel to be kind' adage."

I hear him uncapping the bottle and sipping from it.

"Anyway, according to my mother, she and my father fell in love the first time they met."

Yesterday, that kind of sentence would have sounded far-fetched to me.

"But she rebuffed him. He pursued her. She pretended not to be interested. She says this was the way she thought she was meant to behave. So she made my father propose to her several times, and she kept turning him down."

I hear the unravelling of a chocolate wrapper.

"The truth was, she told me, that although she was keen on my father, she knew that her parents would be angry if she brought home a Christian boyfriend, and would disown her if she brought home a Christian husband, even if he spoke fluent Arabic. But somewhere along the line, in that summer visit, something gave. She came home with me, a shrimp in her belly."

He slips the chocolate bar into my hand. I take a square and give the rest back to him.

"They'd made plans for him to visit Cape Town during his next term break, but when she told him about me, he flew over immediately to join her. They decided not to tell her parents that he was Christian. Besides, who would guess he was a Christian when he came from Iraq and was called Abdullah?"

"Of course, it has to be a Muslim name!"

"Exactly. So they were married by Islamic rites, and after a brief honeymoon that lasted three days, he went back to England to sort out the legal requirements and find a new home for his bride. Only, he never got around to doing any of that. He'd barely been back at college when he got news via a family friend that his father was ill. So he returned to Iraq."

Darya pauses to gulp from the water bottle. I swallow with him.

"My mother never heard from him again. From what she could piece together, he was arrested on his arrival in Iraq. He was one of the many who vanished, the very thing my grandfather had been scared would happen. And no one ever heard from him again."

For a while we don't speak, then I hear the matter-of-fact rustling of the chocolate paper as we pass it back and forth between our fingers.

Eventually he says, "I studied for a while at the college where he'd taught in England. It made him seem real and not a figment of my mother's imagination."

It's strange he should say that, because in this enveloping darkness, I'm beginning to feel that I've conjured him into existence.

I say, "You don't sound English."

"I'm not. I only did a postgrad degree there, so I didn't have time to develop a new accent."

Unlike Precious, who once went on a whistle-stop tour of London and came home sporting a fake English accent along with counterfeit designer denims.

"So you grew up without a dad?"

"Yes and no. My mother remarried and I've always called my stepfather 'Dad'. They married when I was little, and I can't remember a time when he wasn't in my life. I've never felt the absence of a father, but sometimes I've felt an absence of something that I can't describe."

I know what he means.

He says, "I visited Iraq once, a few years ago, after the last war, and met up with my father's extended family, took some photos. Photography's kind of a hobby of mine, although I'm not very good at it. When I look at the photos now, they all seem posed."

"What about your family here?"

"There's my mother, my stepfather and I have a sister, we call her Jay-Jay. I have no idea why. I think it's the toddler name she used when referring to herself, and it stuck. She was born in my matric year, a laatlammetjie."

"You mean your half-sister," I correct automatically. I've never considered my father's ducklings my sisters. We don't have the same mother.

"Genetically? Right. Never thought of it like that. We've always been close, despite our age gap. I stayed with my parents when I was an undergrad, and I'd rush home from classes in time to read my baby sister a story. Although now that she's almost a teenager it does seem that she's rolling her eyes at me *and* our parents. What about you? Do you just have the one sister? Any brothers?"

"No, no brothers." There is another pause while I try to decide whether or not I should tell him about you, Amal. "My sister's dead. At least, she must be. She went missing in my last year of high school. We haven't heard from her since."

My voice trails off. It's funny how, even after all these years, there are times when I can't say these words without wanting to cry.

"Sorry," he says. Then, as though he's determined to sidetrack me, adds, "You smell good."

"It's vanilla. From the cupcakes." I sniff at my clothes.

I hear him shifting forward, inhaling audibly.

"Mmm. But it can't be vanilla essence. My mother's kitchen doesn't smell like that, and she bakes all the time."

"Well, your mother probably uses supermarket vanilla essence. We use the real thing in the shop."

"There's a difference?" He sounds doubtful.

He leans closer again, sniffs at a spot near my neck, under my ear. The darkness tightens around me.

"It's a lovely perfume, you should bottle it."

"I'm sure someone's already done that. Vanilla's supposed

to have aphrodisiac qualities." Oh no, I want to kick myself.

"Really? Tell me more."

"Well, according to legend, the first vanilla orchid can be traced back to a pair of doomed lovers. She was a princess, he was a commoner. They ran away together when her father forbade her to marry him. They were hunted down and decapitated."

"That seems excessive."

"Right, well the place where their heads landed, or rather where the blood that spurted from their bodies touched the earth, is said to be the exact spot where the first vanilla flower bloomed."

"And how does that make it an aphrodisiac, exactly?"

"I don't know." I laugh uncomfortably.

"Vanilla was more of an aphrodisiac before you told me that story!"

We're both quiet, and then he volunteers, "I'm an artist."

A painter. That explains his dirty fingernails. I think of the colourful but dry-as-dust powder we were given my first year at school. The stuff you mix with water just before you throw it all over the skirt of your hideous uniform.

"What do you paint?" I ask.

"Mostly seascapes and some portraits. The sea's always fascinated me. I dabbled with the idea of studying oceanography. But art won."

"So you studied at your dad's college?"

"Yes, and I also studied art here in Cape Town, much to my mother's disappointment – she wanted me to become a doctor."

"Doctors are overrated."

"My mother doesn't agree. Even though I'll be thirty on my next birthday I think she still hopes I'll find a real career."

We're almost the same age.

He says, "I'm going back to university next semester, to do some guest-lecturing in my field. I'm going to be the artist-in-residence at my father's old college."

Then, without preamble, the lights come on and I'm sure he can read the regret on my face. We blink at each other, and then we both look away. The doors slide open with their customary ping. Our gazes lock. He gets up, dusting off those fingers on his jeans.

We walk out of the lift together, into the sunshine of the small lobby, where we continue to blink for a few moments, before he says, "Well, that wasn't so bad. At least I got to meet you." He gestures towards me, palm face-up. "I'll come in and visit next time I walk past your shop."

I smile and give him a small wave, which he returns. He hesitates, then seems to change his mind about something, waves again and leaves through the front doors.

I watch those doors for a few seconds, trying to search for a trace of him, some kind of lingering ectoplasm, but there's nothing. He's gone. Maybe I imagined him.

Then, suddenly, he's back, asking me for my phone number. Amal, perhaps I hesitated, but not for long. Like a woman without a husband, I give him my mobile number, and he returns the favour. Then he bends down as if to kiss me, but surprise and fear make me take a step back. Instead, I walk around him towards the exit, where we turn away from each other and head off in opposite directions.

In my car, there's light spilling everywhere in liquid waves that make me feel as though I'm melting, even with the car's air-conditioning system on high. My skin feels blistery, hot as a new-blown piece of glass, and as malleable. I drive off into daydreams about Darya, and wake up in my parking bay outside the shop to the clicking of knitting needles coming from the backseat. I refuse to turn around to check if Oma's there, but I recognise the purrs that can only belong to Mrs Truffles.

Rakel is packing mint cupcakes behind the sparkling glass counters. She smiles at me as I walk in. "Did you get caught in the blackout?" she asks.

I nod. I tell her I was stuck in a lift.

She says, "How awful. Are you okay?"

She takes off her latex gloves that remind me of Taj and comes towards me to put the back of her hand on my forehead, but I shake my head no and begin to walk towards the kitchen.

Bonny is perched on my baking table typing on her phone. She is surrounded by a cupcake order that should have been boxed by now. When she sees me, she jumps off the table lightly, happily, and waves her phone at me. "My boyfriend sent me a photo of himself." She giggles, and shows me a picture of a young stranger. I've seen her flirting with Kwezi and I half-thought he was her boyfriend.

As Bonny begins to pack the waiting cupcakes into their

boxes and I get the ingredients together for a new batch, she tells me more about her latest admirer. I notice Rakel watching me. Amal, that's when I begin to wonder (absurdly) if she can hear my thoughts about the man in the lift. I become flustered and forget to add sugar to the batter until Rakel hands it to me, looking at me with her eyes narrowed like she's trying to see into my soul.

I go home a little later than usual and, again, I'm not sure how I do it: the car seems to be on autopilot. At least I don't have to cook supper. When Taj is around, he cooks, lots of vegetables, organic, of course, plenty of salads and white meat, dhals and low-GI pastas. When he's not around, Precious and I live on takeaways from the local chicken place. Tonight, according to my nose, it's some kind of pasta. I kick off my shoes at the front door and walk on bare feet towards the kitchen. I can hear Taj's deep voice in conversation and the higher-pitched slightly hysterical one Precious uses when he's happy. For some reason, the sound of their voices, the sound of my normal domestic life, fills me with guilt and sadness. It bewilders me. It's not as though I've done anything wrong. As I get to the kitchen door, Taj comes out of the room, wiping his hands on a blue-and-white chequered dishcloth, chatting into his phone, which is held under his chin. His hair is wet, and there's a price tag hanging from his shirt cuff.

"Be kind," he mouths at me, gesturing with his head back through the kitchen door.

"Why?" I whisper, but he doesn't answer.

"Yes, of course, I understand," he says into the phone. To me he murmurs, "You'll see. I'm on my way to the hospital."

In the kitchen, the remnants of a plate of food lie in front of Precious and he's looking at the screen of his notebook with the rapturous gaze a mother reserves for her firstborn. We usually only see his computer when he needs to pretend to his parents that he's working on his degree. He's worked on that degree through three or four laptops. I reach over him for a plate and dish up some food, before coming to stand next to him, then swallow my first mouthful of spaghetti without chewing.

"What's this?" I ask.

"A site for designing a bride."

What if Darya's married?

"*Designing* a bride? Don't you mean designing a bride's dress?" I say.

"No, it's more like a site for *choosing* a bride."

"Internet dating?" I eat a forkful of food.

"No, not exactly."

"A mail-order bride?" I poke his shoulder with the back of my fork. "You're buying a bride? Does your mother know about her new daughter-in-law?"

"I'm going to call her Jalebi," he responds, ignoring my question.

"Doesn't she have a name of her own? And why on earth would you name her after a piece of sweetmeat?"

"During our more intimate moments, I'll call her Jella-Bibi."

I take a deep breath, then another, the way Alice has shown us to do before we start writing.

"Malak," he says, "put on your specs and help me with this."

"With what?"

"Choosing her finer details. You have to tick off your preferences." He gestures towards the computer screen. "Taj was going to help, but then he got a call from the hospital."

"Precious, what are you talking about?"

"Just get your glasses and you'll see. This is a site for building a woman."

"I didn't know women could be built." I put down my plate of food and find my spectacles in my handbag. The blurry photographs on the web page transform themselves into unbelievable images. "You want me to help you choose a sex doll!"

"She's not just a sex doll. I think of Jalebi more as an inanimate friend. And bride. This process of choosing her isn't very different from the arranged marriage my mother has been trying to get me to agree to for the last decade. Anyway, I don't need your approval. I need your expertise." He lifts his chin towards the screen in an almost pitiful gesture. "I want you to help me choose her."

"Why me?"

"You're a woman. I need help choosing her clothes."

"I'm not exactly a fashionista."

"Yes, but you're a girl. You wear women's clothes."

The website appears to be based in North America. Oma used to say that's where the Shaytan spends most of his time, remember, Amal? It seems she was right.

Precious is offered two body sizes. He chooses the bigger version. His doll weighs in at thirty-one kilograms. He splurges an additional $50 for a bigger bra cup. The options for her face include several goddesses from the entertainment industry, which all appear to have been carved by the hand of the same cosmetic surgeon. But there are also faces that look like ordinary women. In fact, Amal, Precious lingers over a face that could almost be yours if you were made of silicone. But his mouse clicks on another, which comes in "Asian" skin tone. Then we have a long debate over eye colour.

"Blue or violet?" I suggest toad-green. He chooses violet with matching eye shadow and heavy black kohl. I watch him tick off nail-varnish colour (fluorescent pink) for her well-rounded talons, and a matching shade for her lips, which look like they'll need a litre of lipstick.

He asks my advice on the hair colour. We argue about this and I threaten to withdraw my help. I say, "Brunette, with that skin tone," but he wants platinum. He finally chooses raspberry-coloured, hip-length hair. How will she wash it? I wonder.

I begin to scrape at my congealed food and nibble at a piece of squishy spaghetti.

Next, Precious has a choice of the vagina attachment style – permanent or removable. I wonder why every woman doesn't come with this option. He pays an extra $40 for her to be waxed, like a good Muslim girl.

The site claims she'll arrive dressed in a "whisper of a nightgown, her own perfume and cleansing lotion".

Then Precious buys a wardrobe that he doesn't consult me on at all. It consists of a pair of fishnet tights, a red micro-skirt, a black lacy bra, a pair of thongs, and thigh-high calfskin boots. The sort of clothes Mum would call common.

We have another argument. I say if he wanted to dress her like Hooker Barbie, why did he need my advice? He says her clothes aren't a reflection of her personality, they're just what's fashionable.

He clicks "Send", and Jalebi's specifications fly off into cyber-space.

Precious smiles at me and says, "I've just bought myself an anatomically correct doll."

"Why is it that 'anatomically correct' has nothing to do with her brain or her heart?" I ask Precious.

He ignores my question, and says, "Maybe I'm tired of objectifying organic women. It will be different with a doll, won't it? She's a fantasy."

"No, she's an object that you're objectifying."

"But she's not an object to herself because she isn't a self."

"Then why have you given her a name? Isn't it because you're going to pretend she's your girlfriend?"

"No, Malak, not unless she cooks for me."

"Very funny."

"Malak, you know my mother's been trying to arrange a marriage for me for years. At least, this way, I get to choose my own ... er ... interim partner."

"Your doll's a hugely expensive sex toy."

"I'm hoping she'll be more than that."

"What are you going to do with her when you go through

one of your religious phases? You know, when you flush all your dagga away and swear that you'll never smoke the stuff again and promise to pray five times a day?"

He grins, and says, "That only happens when I've smoked something cheap and I'm suffering from paranoia. Or delusions."

"Or both."

"Or both," he agrees.

I leave Precious to fantasise over his dream woman, cute and mute forever, and go out to the balcony to watch the end of the sunset. On the evening breeze, I can hear the shrieks of children, the sound of water splashing. Perched on the branch of a nearby tree, there's a cat waiting for a bird to fly home to an abandoned nest.

I have to tell you, Amal, that usually February is my favourite month. Well, aside from Valentine's Day. I especially love the balmy evenings, but tonight February's magic isn't working. Maybe I should go for a walk, but then walking alone at night makes me feel vulnerable. (I'm sure I'd feel a lot safer if I could leave my vagina at home like Jalebi.) Perhaps I should go for a ride on my neglected exercise bike.

But even after forty-five tedious minutes on the bike, I find it impossible to sleep. It's because of Darya. I can't get him off my mind and it's perplexing. I keep thinking about things I should have said, instead of the silly things I did say. I doubt if you ever had those moments, Amal. You were always so confident, even when we met strangers, whereas I'd hide in your shadow. If only you were here to advise me now. But, of course, if you were here, I wouldn't be in this predicament. I wouldn't be the one married to Taj.

Amal, I can't even remember how you and Taj met. I know you were still in high school. All I remember is you coming home and saying you'd met the man you were going to marry. I know I felt irritated and jealous that someone else was getting your attention. When I met Taj, I remember thinking how ordinary he was, and I couldn't imagine why you'd want to marry him. Did you think about Taj all the time the way I am thinking about Darya?

My circular thoughts are interrupted by an sms from Darya inviting me for lunch on Saturday. I'm so happy to hear from him that I almost agree before remembering that I work on Saturdays. And that I'm married. We send each other a series of text-negotiations, during which time I'm tempted to call him, but I'm overcome with nerves. What if I become a prisoner of my tongue again? Eventually our texts arrange a Tuesday dinner (Taj and Precious have an audience with Shireen every Tuesday) at a Turkish place he likes.

I've just turned off my phone when Taj gets home, and since I'm awake he imagines I'm feeling amorous. During Taj's final spasms, I think of Darya and the text messages we've exchanged.

The next morning I'm at work well before Rakel, so that by the time she arrives there are already dozens of angel cupcakes waiting to be decorated. Rakel is in one of her cheerful moods, which I only appreciate when I'm in a similar disposition. Today I find her irritating.

But that's because I'm regretting that I agreed to go to dinner with Darya. Not because I don't want to see him, Amal, but because I'm afraid of seeing him. Tuesday is both terrifyingly close and as distant as Mars. It's also after the fuss of Valentine's Day. Not that I'm complaining about work. It's a great distraction. But even in my busiest moments, Darya is here with me, like wallpaper or background music, unobtrusive, but curling around the edges of my day.

Darya's builders have asked for another extension, so he's staying on at Madame's. He says he's preparing for his teaching course, which begins in April. I have never been interested in art, but now I find myself browsing the Internet for his paintings of the sea, when I should be piping hearts onto chocolate cupcakes. Amal, the paintings I've seen, of sea and sky merging, of struggling rocks, of stretches of empty sand, remind me of you. There's one with an empty shell in the foreground that looks so forlorn it makes me weepy.

The restaurant we meet at is close to Alice's bookshop. He's already seated when I get there, watching the door, which unbalances me. He stands up when I reach the table, says hello, and hands me a menu as I sit down and slip my handbag between my ankles. He looks different from the picture of him I've been carrying around in my head, and perhaps he's thinking the same thing, because he doesn't stop looking at me.

I glance around the restaurant, glad of its too-loud music, aware that his eyes are still on my face. There are several tables, and only two are empty of diners. The waitresses are dressed in belly-dancing costumes, their navels filled with jewels, and their arms heavily laden with bangles, which tinkle every time they move. They remind me of Clarissa from my writing class, although their wardrobe is more Jalebi-like. I tell myself that, even if my marriage feels fake, this is not a date. Maybe if I can force myself to believe that, my palms will stop feeling sticky. Even my feet feel tingly and damp.

He asks loudly over the background of drums and something that sounds like a wailing baby but may be a clarinet, "What are you having to drink?" I murmur "water", like I'm a child afraid of speaking up. He gets up to pour us two glasses of water from a jug placed on a corner table. When he returns with the water, I notice two mint leaves floating on its surface. He sits down, opens the menu and I do the same. While we read over the contents, he makes suggestions, as he's been here before, but he tells me that he's vegetarian, so he can't recommend the meat dishes. I find myself not really listening to him but watching his mouth and the way he uses his hands all the time when he speaks, almost knocking over his water glass at one point.

The bejewelled waitress appears to take our orders. I'm torn for a moment between being polite and not ordering meat, but then I submit to my carnivore urges.

"How long have you been in the cupcake business?"

"Ever since I left varsity."

"But why cupcakes?"

He's watching me all the time, and I can't keep a grip on my thoughts. So I look down at his hands, which are now resting on the table. Maybe if I can't see his face I'll be able to concentrate.

"It was Rakel's idea. Her home business was expanding and she needed a shop and a partner, and that's where I came in."

Looking at his hands doesn't help. I want to touch them.

"Do you like what you do?"

"Yes. Mostly. And you?"

"Absolutely. I've always wanted to do something artistic, although I didn't know I'd end up a painter. Now I've even learnt to enjoy teaching art classes, though teaching never held much interest for me before. But today I was excited about preparing my lessons. I want my students to feel as happy as I am when I paint."

"I don't know much about art," I say. "Actually, all I know is that Picasso's squiggles are horribly expensive, a musician whose name I can't remember sang a sad song about Van Gogh, and I'd recognise Frida Kahlo's unibrow anywhere."

Now at least he'll know how ignorant I am.

"Hey, Kahlo's one of the artists who influenced me."

"Well, I know she was into self-portraits, which to me seems a bit narcissistic, but then why'd she refuse to pluck that unibrow?"

"Beauty's in the eye of the beholder."

We stare at each other, and my throat goes dry when he smiles at me.

The waitress with her melodic jewellery appears with our food. The food on my plate looks unrecognisable and his appears to have far too much beige and green in it.

As I manoeuvre my food around my plate, I wonder how

this happened, and what the hell I'm doing eating strange food in a strange restaurant with a strange man. Then I look up, and he's smiling at me again, and it seems that this is the only place I should be. Not with Taj and our substitute arranged marriage, not even with Mum, not when I'll never be you, Amal.

We start to eat, but I can't taste the food. It sticks in my throat and I find myself reaching for the water all the time. Then he tells me something about his dead grandfather, and I tell him about Oma. How she'd left a mediaeval town in Europe, famous for the selling of my favourite cheese, to accompany her five older brothers to the diamond-dusty town of Kimberley, where they were determined to find their fortunes. Where they promptly did just that, although four of them also found Death, in some odd disguises, during the ten years they lived in that dream-driven place.

Darya says it sounds like my ancestors lived interesting lives.

I tell him how, when Oma got to Kimberley, the second Boer War had not been over for long, but the lust for instant wealth made many not directly involved in the carnage over-look the war in the hope that finding a diamond sitting in the dirt of the sieve would make death and backbreaking work worthwhile.

He shakes his head. But I don't pause to interpret the gesture in case I forget how to talk.

I tell him that Oma said Kimberley always felt bright to her. She wasn't sure if that was because of the diamond fever, or because it was the first city to have electrical streetlights.

And there Oma met our great-grandfather, fresh off the boat from Surat. Like her brothers, he had also come to find his fortune. It was one of those brothers who brought her future husband home. Oma read his teacup and saw a burnished diamond shining at the bottom of it. A month later they were married.

"What does that mean?" Darya interrupts, and uses the interjection to order coffee. "Does that mean she married him for his future fortune?"

"No, I promise you, theirs was a love story. I have my mother's word that Oma was in love with her husband up until the day she died."

"And your mother doesn't lie?" He raises his left eyebrow along with his coffee cup. "No." I take a sip of the bitter coffee, then another of water.

"I'll be sure to ask her that when we meet," he says.

And I'll be sure you never meet my mother, is my silent response.

By now we've agreed on dessert, apricots filled with thick cream and almonds.

I watch him pop one into his mouth with his hand, and I'm pleased to see that his fingernails look cleaner tonight.

I tell him, Amal, that at the end of a decade of strenuous work, Oma and her husband and surviving brother were wealthy enough to pack their trunks and return to her husband's homeland, for which he was pining. There Opa set up a small diamond-polishing business, employing his relatives. Oma and

Opa stayed on for almost twenty years, with Oma immersing herself in yet another new culture and several new languages. But when she was in her late forties, her husband decided it was time they returned to South Africa.

He had spent a few days in Cape Town on his way to Kimberley, and had liked the combination of sea and mountain. So they sold their business to her brother, who in the interim had married one of Opa's cousins, and set sail for Cape Town. On the way over, Oma was seasick for the first time in her life. She continued to be plagued by nausea on land. Once they'd found a place to live, close to where Opa could indulge in his passion for Table Mountain, Oma went off to the local doctor.

"I know, your Oma was pregnant."

"Yes. How'd you guess? The way my Mum tells it, Oma's pregnancy was the biggest shock of her life."

"So your Oma gave birth to your granny. What was she like?" he asks, finally stirring a half teaspoon of brown sugar into the bitter brew he's drinking.

"I'm not really sure. She and my grandfather died before I was born."

"What's with the people in your family dying all the time?" He reaches out and moves a strand of hair out of my eye. Has he wanted to touch me as much as I've wanted to touch him?

He sees my face, and says, "Sorry, that was a stupid thing to say. Anyway, dying's what people do."

I tell him about the car accident in which our grandparents passed away, and my childhood neurosis about traffic lights. He tells me about how terrified he was of learning to swim, which is why his mother got him interested in drawing the sea in the hope that it would help him overcome his fear.

Talking to him about Oma has made me forget all about my sweaty hands, but then he says, "So your great-grandparents had the briefest of courtships. I like that. Have you ever wanted to marry someone after a first date?"

The soles of my feet begin to tingle again.

"No."

"Have you been on many first dates?"

"Not really." I put my hands in my lap so he can't see them trembling.

"And you've never wanted to get married?"

I slowly shake my head from side to side and again he reaches over to fix my hair again. I sit back out of reach, but he moves forward, tucking the hair behind my ear, catching my earlobe between his fingers, his eyes on my mouth.

"So you've never been serious about a boyfriend?"

"No." How to explain to him that I've never been in love, but I have a husband?

"There must have been someone."

"Mmm, yes, sort of, but he was more interested in my sister."

"Did he get to know you so he could get closer to your sister?"

"Something like that."

"And what happened when she went missing?"

"I don't think he got over her. I imagine he's still in love with her."

He looks at me squarely.

"Are you in love with him?"

I don't have to pretend shock.

"No, not at all."

I realise with a small pang of something like disappointment that this is the truth.

Darya sits back, smiling at me.

"Good, I'm glad. You were making me jealous there for a moment. When can we meet again?"

"We're still meeting, aren't we?" I gesture to the table and the restaurant. "This isn't over yet."

"But I need to know when we're going to see each other after tonight."

I look down at the table and the serviette I've twisted into red-and-white fragments.

He reaches over for a few pieces of the broken napkin and says it looks like I've made confetti, then weaves his fingers into mine.

After our dinner, he walks me to my car, taking my hand in his, and tries to persuade me to meet with him the next night. But the evening has been overwhelming enough and I tell him I'm going away to Mum for a few days. I open the car and stand behind the driver's door, drawing it towards me like a shield. He takes my right hand, thanks me for sharing dinner, and kisses the tips of my fingers, ensuring my pitch forward into disaster. He comes closer, as though to kiss me properly, but I slide down into the car seat and shut the door.

That night, driving home from the restaurant, I realise I've just experienced my first date. And I also remember that the next day is my wedding anniversary.

Tips for Surrogate Wives

Rakel and Barbara are discussing something political, but I can't concentrate on what they're saying because my brain is buzzing with thoughts of Darya. The more I see of him, the more I crave him. I am beginning to feel about Darya the way Precious does about his weed. I think I've only ever felt this way about men in books. Alice's calm voice brings me to the present.

She says, "There may be more than one identity in an auto-biography. There is the I who lived in the past and there is the I who is writing the story in the present. How do you write about yourself? Let's try. I want you to look at the photo you were asked to bring along and write about yourself in the third person. Your prompt is 'She who …'"

I glance at Rakel's photo. It's one I've seen often before. It was taken with her second husband, on their wedding day. She loved him best of all, she says, even though he was a dull lover. Rakel's photo is black and white, which emphasises her dark hair and eyes.

Do you recall, Amal, that when I was little I thought black

and white photos meant that in the world before our birth, before my memory, people had lived with only those two shades? And it was only with our births that colour had arrived in the world. I remember suggesting this to you. I remember how you pushed your lips to one side of your face, your thoughtful look, and then nodded, telling me I was definitely right. That was one of my proudest childhood moments.

Rakel's photograph is pristine behind its glass frame, while mine's grubby from living in my purse for several years. It was taken early in my matric year, at a fancy-dress party you dragged me to. I don't know whose party it was, probably someone you'd met at varsity. You made so many friends that first year, went to so many parties, it was a wonder you got any studying done. I found the photo when Mum was moving out of the house, after I was married, and was struck by its melancholy. But then everything after your vanishing had the colour of melancholy, the gloomy shade of a dismal Sunday evening when you know you have to be at school the next day.

In the photograph you're dressed as Dorothy from *The Wizard of Oz*, in pigtails tied with red ribbons, and ruby slippers. If only, like Dorothy, you'd found your way home again. You stare at the camera, your smile a shine of lipstick, one hand interlaced with Taj's Tin-Man fingers, the other clasping the furry arm of my Cowardly Lion costume. Precious grins from my side, the straw stuffing of his brain dangling down to his shoulders like ridiculous earrings. Taj's smile is broad too. I can't remember seeing him that happy since you left. His silver face-paint makes him gleam like one of those glow-in-the dark condoms Precious was handing out at the party. It's strange how many memories a single photograph can evoke.

I'm staring back at the camera, unsmiling. There's a slice of chocolate cake on my lap. I remember I didn't want to dress up in that stupid costume. I remember it itched. But when I refused to go you pouted and said I was being selfish. You said Precious wouldn't have a partner if I didn't agree to go with. Of course I knew you and Taj needed me there to distract Precious or you'd never have time alone with each other. I can't remember whose party it was or where it was held, but each time I see that photo I taste the cake on my tongue. Chocolate-mousse-melt-in-the-mouth softness. I've never eaten one like it again. In the photograph, we all look like spanking new versions of ourselves.

Alice's egg timer tells us it's time to stop. I've been staring at the photograph all this time and my unspoilt page looks back at me vacantly. When I told Taj about the writing classes, he bought me a journal with thick creamy sheets and an orange leather cover. He also bought me a pen whose ink, when I use it to write on these pages, fades to the consistency and colour of dried blood. I had hoped Taj's expensive writing paper and pen would form a synaptic link with my brain, and the words would proceed down from my mind to the paper directly without involving my consciousness. That my memoir would write itself. Sadly, that hasn't happened. Writing is hard.

Now Alice asks for a volunteer to read the writing assignment, and Clarissa's hand shoots up before Alice's question mark has time to form itself in the air. Clarissa holds up her photograph. The woman in it is wearing a Mona Lisa expression, the kind Shireen is always trying to achieve, because "smiling ages a woman". Clarissa begins to read. Her voice booms at us as if we're seated in the last row of a huge theatre and not within pinching distance of her.

She who lies sleepless and waits and longs for her daddy to come home so she can sing him the song she's written for him. She who stands on the school's stage in the spotlight and feels the applause in the cells of her scalp. She who goes to her first audition and gets a job painting scenery. She who becomes the understudy. She who places a marble strategically, where it will cause the most damage. She who takes her first bow, with her first bouquet, from her first beau. She who performs to acclaim. She who is a bride and then a mother. She who signs autographs after being a corpse in a small film that is seen in faraway places. She whose face appears on the covers of magazines, which she buys by the dozens. She who secretly watches herself on screen in the dark. She, who is ageing, is also she who always waits for the applause of her daddy.

The next morning my mind keeps wandering back to Clarissa's story, but then I forget it as the shop gets noisier. You'd think March would be a slow month for cupcakes after the madness of February, but you'd be wrong. Everyone in Cape Town seems to have a birthday in March (subtract nine months and you'll find yourself in winter, which is a very wet season in the Cape).

This year March is especially busy for me, because I'm juggling two men. It's not that hard, really. Technology makes it easy to stay in touch with a partner outside of marriage, and it helps when the partner inside of the marriage has a hectic job and a busy extracurricular schedule.

There are days when Taj and I don't even see each other. I only know he's been home because I find a damp towel peering at me from the laundry basket or see a half-eaten plate of food in the kitchen sink. Of course the plate could belong to Precious. Or to a particularly intelligent cockroach. If they can live without their heads for seven days, what else are they capable of?

Darya has been involved in research for his classes, Art and Health, or something like that, but we've managed to see each other a few times, always in public places, which means we've never done more than hold hands and he hasn't tried to kiss me again. I wonder if he's afraid he's misread my interest. When we're apart I keep fantasising about us doing a whole lot more than holding hands. I imagine that the next time I see him the first thing I'll do is kiss him. But when I'm with him I become immobile. I'm afraid. I'm scared of how I want to be closer to him and what that means for me, for us, for the future. So, for now, it's just been coffee dates and dinners. He thinks my hours at work are much longer than they really are, and I've also led him to believe that I live with Rakel, which means I don't have much privacy.

Today I'm making four dozen spiders with chocolate abdomens and liquorice legs for a kiddie's birthday party, so I have plenty of time to think about my so-called memoir while I'm decorating. When I began writing this, it was going to be all about you, Amal, about your disappearance, but somewhere along the way I've got lost too. Or maybe I'm just taking the long way through the woods.

You're not in my past, because you're my constant companion, Amal. Even if our conversations are one-sided, I visit you all the time in my dreams. Sometimes, after I've dreamt of you, I wake up thinking the dream is reality, your disappearance a nightmare.

Mum's been around for a visit. She stayed for a few nights while she was sorting out the arrangements for her travel documents. (She really is going to Canada, I still can't believe it.) I had to haul out several dozens of books and store them temporarily at Rakel's to make space for her in the spare room. Taj, as usual, was absent for most of her stay, but he did turn up on her last night, and we all went out for dinner to a local Indian place that Precious insists has the most authentic cuisine.

As usual, there was an awkward silence between Taj and Mum which, thankfully, was filled by Precious. The years he has spent as a student means he always has something to talk about. Sometimes it's hard to reconcile Precious, the academic, with Precious, the man who ordered a sex doll off the Internet. But then, Amal, you were the one who always said Precious was eccentric. You often told me stories about his funny behaviour, like the tricks he developed to avoid Shireen and her ideas on how a proper son should behave. I know that Shireen often held up Taj as an example of what a good son should be, but I also know that Precious never took that example too seriously. He certainly didn't hold it against Taj. I'll just have to think of Jalebi as a mail-order bride. In Taj's extended family there have been a few such marriages and Russian brides seem to be the most fashionable, especially with older men who couldn't manage to be proper husbands or fathers during their first marriages, and are now pretending they can be both with younger foreign women. In a way, Dad did something similar, Amal, didn't he? And he seems happy. I think Liesbet has helped him get over your disappearance.

The dinner with Mum turned out to be a surprisingly happy event, and that night I took a cup of hot chocolate into her room before she went to bed.

"Do you know this is my first time flying alone?" Mum asked. "I've never travelled without Oma or your father before."

"Are you anxious about it?"

"Yes." Mum sipped at the chocolate, then returned it to the bedside table. She was working on a memory quilt. "A little. I know it's silly of me but it feels strange to be going on a long journey on my own. I keep imagining what will happen if the plane crashes. What will happen to my quilts."

Who would be there to wait for Amal?

"That's probably why I brought this one along," she pointed to the quilt. "I want to make sure it's complete before I leave. In case I don't come back."

"Mum, what's this? Are you having a premonition?"

"No!" Mum protested, and then laughed. It was a strange, almost irreverent sound. I can count on one hand the number of times I've heard Mum laugh since you've been gone, Amal, and that's not my attempt at hyperbole.

"No, I'm just nervous about leaving my home for such a long time. Sara's suggested I stay with her for six months, and I keep wondering, what if we get on each other's nerves? Neither of us has lived with someone else for years."

"Well, you don't have to stay that long, you could always come up with an excuse to leave early. You could say you miss home. I'm sure she'll understand. She knows you haven't been away from home since—" I fluffed up the pillows behind Mum's back and I used the movement to change the end of my sentence.

"She knows you haven't been away from home for a long time."

"You're right, I'm being silly. It's going to be wonderful to meet Sara face to face and I'm sure we'll cope with the living arrangements."

Mum shrugged and then said she'd have to let the future take care of itself. She went back to her quilting. I said goodnight and returned to my room where Taj was already asleep.

That night I dreamt you and I were at the beach near Mum's house. The water as usual was talkative, like it was unburdening itself to a long-suffering friend. In my dream, Amal, you were floating on your back out to sea. I was on something soft, buoyant atop the waves, lying back, my legs in the water till midcalf. The bits of my body that were in the water were frozen. But the parts of me that were out of the water were feverish. There was something nibbling at my right foot and I sat up, peered down, waved the dark water aside, and saw a fish snacking on the dead skin of my heel. It looked up at me with its fishy eyes, opened its fishy mouth, and in a deep voice said, *I'm ready to die now.* Then it flopped out of the water and into my lap where it lay, waiting. Obediently, I unzipped its body. Blood and entrails fell into my lap along with fishy eggs. Nestling among its innards was your bloated engagement ring, diamonds, rubies and emeralds.

Amal, I said, *look what I've found.*

You didn't appear to hear me. You were moving out to sea on your back, your eyes open, your hair spilling around you, my sister-Ophelia.

I woke up to the memory of you and Dad dutifully inviting me along on that last camping trip. But, of course, as usual, I declined. I knew you wanted to be alone with each other on what would be the last camping trip you two would take before your marriage. If I'd gone with, would you still be here, Amal?

You went to your favourite nature reserve. You were sharing a tent, as usual, there were early spring flowers out, as usual, and it was cold, as usual. That's what Dad kept saying afterwards: everything was the way it usually was. You arrived in the late afternoon. You set up camp. You went for a walk. You had supper together. Afterwards, you played cards together. You both read a little. You spoke about the impending wedding. You both went to sleep.

In the morning, Dad woke up to find he was alone. The jersey you'd borrowed from me was spread out over your sleeping bag, the only farewell I got.

The policeman in charge looked like a heavyweight boxer and was called Koos, and for a while he was suspicious of Dad, Taj and even Precious. Koos worked on your case for long hours. He never gave up, and Mum and him became close friends. But, despite his determination, he could not find evidence to link anyone, stranger or family, to your vanishing. Koos still visits Mum, although he's been retired for several years. She gave him the gift of a remembrance quilt when his life partner died.

Once you were gone, everyone asked questions. Had you gone hiking by yourself that night after bed? Impossible, said Dad, you would never be that irresponsible. Could you have gone for an early-morning walk and got lost? No, no, no! said Dad. You knew the area well. And you wouldn't have left without your cellphone.

They reasoned that you went walking along the cliff's edge, lost your footing on a loose stone and slipped to your death in the waters below. They found no trace of you.

The winter you vanished there were two similar disappearances in the area. One before you, and one after. Both the other girls were around twelve years old. Koos decided there was a serial killer on the loose. He determined that because of your physique, you'd been mistaken for a younger girl. Koos was certain there was a paedophile preying in the area. Over the next three years there were more disappearances that fit the profile of this possible serial murderer. Then nothing.

They've never found you or those other missing little girls. Their only connection to you is that their vanishings were perfect too. No car tyre prints, no piece of cloth trapped by a twig of a tree, not a strand of hair, no trace of blood under a suspect's nail, not even a real suspect.

Amal, have I mentioned to you that since your disappearance I've become obsessed with crime stories? At first I only read novels, but later Precious got me hooked on a TV detective series too. Once, Precious and I spent seventy-two hours holed up at home watching a programme that had first aired over a decade before, around the time you went missing. Taj was inadvertently to blame for fuelling my new addiction. That was the year he'd convinced me to go on a trip with him. He was going to give a paper at a conference and after much persuasion I agreed. I know it's silly of me, but I've always had this ridiculous superstition that if I'm away there'll be news of you. As soon as he heard we were going away, Precious invited himself along. We were supposed to have left for New York for six days, but at the last minute Taj cancelled because of an emergency. A patient of his had gone into premature labour with twins. She lost one of the babies. Which makes her sound careless, but you understand it's not like she misplaced the baby; it's just language's way of saying the baby died.

During our marathon session, we watched the characters maturing and their hairstyles and clothes changing. We watched them growing naturally old, then unnaturally younger, we watched them obsessing about their personal dilemmas (adopting a child, having an abortion, getting married or divorced, moving house, dealing with illness), and we watched them take up new hobbies and lovers. Above all, we watched them solve every crime and find every criminal they needed to with supreme efficiency and endless wisecracks. Missing girls did not remain lost, even if their bodies were found chopped up into gritty bits of bone and slivers of flesh – they were all found and their murderers brought to book.

In the first few weeks after your disappearance, I ate a lot, Amal. I ate for two, the way a pregnant woman is supposed to. I convinced myself that if I ate to bursting point, if I was too stuffed to move, if I ate so much that my lungs were pushing up into my throat and I couldn't breathe, this meant that wherever you were, you weren't hungry. And if you weren't hungry, there was a good chance that you were safe. There was plenty of food around, brought over by our concerned, busybody relatives. In between these dishes, I'd snack on white bread filled with mango atchar from Mum's rapidly dwindling stock. She never made mango atchar again after you went away. Maybe I wouldn't have squandered it if I'd known that.

You vanished during the school holidays, but after you were gone I skipped school until the last term, when I went back to write exams. For several months, I filled my days with clock-watching. I went to bed every evening at 6 pm (with one of the many pills the doctors prescribed Mum) and woke up every morning at 6 am. Sleeping for twelve hours meant I only had to fill twelve hours of the day. I began to walk, around and around the block where our house stood. That bizarre mini-pilgrimage had to last exactly eighty-eight minutes. I don't know why I chose that particular number. Then I allocated myself twenty-five minutes for morning bathroom detail and dressing. Thirty-seven minutes for breakfast and reading every piece in the newspaper for news of you. I checked the lost and found columns and the obituaries in case no one had told us you'd died. Then I gave myself another thirteen minutes for rereading the paper in the hope that I'd missed something. Fifty-five minutes for searching the Internet. This meant that there were another seven hundred and twenty minutes to fill. Seven minutes for watching Mum gaze at the phone and smoke a ciggie. Thirteen minutes for watching Dad trying to get Mum to eat something. Twenty-nine minutes for answering calls from relatives after Mum had picked up the phone in hope, and handed it to me in disgust when it wasn't you.

How many minutes were left? I'm afraid I can't remember the precise number anymore, although once I lived my life mapped out to those minutes, to the ticking of the clock in my head. Each minute, each second, turning you into a memory, making you a part of the past. Or was it you that had turned *me* into a memory? Had you forged a new future for yourself without me in it?

I remember, I spent a lot of time cleaning the house, especially the toilet. After you went, we had visitors all the time and not all the men, not even Dad, sat down to pee, so there were sloshes to clean up off the floor and around the sides of the bowl. You may not know this, Amal, but if you really want to clean under the brim, where those garrulous cartoon-advertisement germs lurk, then believe me, liquid, even in a cleverly designed bottle, doesn't work. You have to use your fingers, your hands, which, of course, means you have to wear rubbery gloves. I spent a lot of time worrying about blind people, who couldn't see the images on TV, who couldn't see just how evil toilet germs looked. And how they loitered. I imagined I could shed quite a few minutes of my day if I volunteered to clean the toilet bowls of blind people. But, of course, even as I tried to punish myself with mundane domestic tasks, there was no getting away from the fact that you were missing and that Mum was blind to everything else.

It's as if Dad and Mum were only ever able to imprint on you, Amal. I was an unwanted, if necessary, spare. But you were the bond that held us together. I remember when we were little, Dad would come home and say, "Girls, what did you do at school today?" And you'd say, "Made a house out of a pump-kin." And he'd say, "Amal, you're so talented." And I'd start to say something, but by then he'd have lost focus, and he'd turn to me and say, "That's nice, dear."

Then I had to return to school for my exams. I remember the pointing fingers and how people would stop speaking the moment I walked into a class. Exams were useful. They ate up several hours a day until school became part of my past too. Around the middle of January, I got a letter to say I'd been accepted at the university. Looking at the date of the letter, I realised my birthday, our birthdays, had come and gone. I knew then that you were dead, Amal. You might have discarded Taj, forsaken Dad, abandoned Mum, but you would never have ignored my birthday. You were gone. You'd vacated the chamber of my heart in which you'd lived from the time before I was born. You were gone without a goodbye. In that place where you'd lived, Amal, I put up a do-not-disturb sign, and I tiptoed out of my emotional world.

So when the suggestion of marrying Taj first arose, I didn't feel surprised or happy. By then nothing mattered anymore. And later, when Mum and Dad called me over to tell me about Dad's impending marriage to Liesbet and Mum's move to be closer to the site of your disappearance, it didn't touch me. None of it had anything to do with you coming back, which was the only thing that I cared about, because a part of me had left the world with you.

Mum didn't seem to mind about Dad remarrying. In fact, she seemed relieved, and she'd been married to him for over two decades, so what right did I have to complain? I was just his daughter and not even his favourite one.

Nor am I Shireen's favourite daughter-in-law. You are, even though you never got to marry Taj. I wonder if Shireen ever told you how she breastfed Taj along with Precious? She loves to remind people of her saintly act. If we're having tea at a family function and some unsuspecting person asks her to hand over the milk jug, she'll do it with a sigh.

"Milk," she'll say, in a stage whisper, "is so important for a baby." Then she'll say even louder, "You know, when my sister died in childbirth, I breastfed Taj along with my Precious. It was just the right thing to do. Now look at him, a doctor!" And everyone will turn dutifully to admire Taj's six-foot, dark-haired Bollywood beauty and know that without Shireen's breast milk he'd have been a scrawny underachiever.

"They're milk brothers," she'll continue, "and if one of them had been a girl they wouldn't have been able to get married, the Qur'an says. Although, of course, I would never have allowed that. I don't approve of cousins getting married. Besides, if that were possible what would have happened to you, Malak?"

That's usually when she turns to me and offers a fake smile that draws everyone's attention to me. Then she'll ask, "Have you met Taj's first wife Malak?"

I don't really mind, Amal. Perhaps because she's been a bride more than once, Shireen believes a daughter-in-law is a visitor in the family. Mostly I'll smile, pretending not to have heard her snide adjective. I'll smile and think, Of course you had enough milk for two babies, you're a bitch. Anyway, according to Precious, milk brothers are men who've screwed the same women simultaneously or consecutively.

Sometimes I wish I was the one who disappeared and not the one left to be your understudy.

If Uncle Santa's around he'll usually start chatting to me about his latest toy and soon everyone's forgotten about me. He's really nice. Did you know she left Precious's father, Adam, for the greener pastures of Uncle Santa's bank balance after Adam was picked up at the local airport with a suitcase full of mandrax? This was back in the seventies, when almost everyone coming home from a visit to India brought back drug-souvenirs. Adam spent several years in prison, and Shireen wiped him and the entire low-class incident (her words) out of her memory. But, of course you, must know all of this, Amal. After all, you and Taj were engaged to be married.

But what you may not know is that after serving jail time, Adam went back to India and this time returned with a medical degree. It was the ornate work of a clever copy machine and a gifted calligraphy artist, and to this day it ensures him a permanent income somewhere in our country's interior. I know this because Precious and his father are in regular contact, though he keeps this a secret from Shireen.

As for Uncle Santa, I rarely see him. Like his namesake, he only comes out on special occasions. I'm convinced Shireen stores him in a cupboard after removing his batteries. Months, years can go by without me remembering his existence and then suddenly there'll be a wedding or an Eid and I'll see him and think that man is a familiar stranger, like someone you recognise from TV. Then I'll remember it's Uncle Santa. He doesn't really look like Santa Claus, but he's always got a new toy to show off to the kids in the family. Lately, his business has gone retro, with faux wooden Jacob's ladders, marble runs, cars, and dolls. I have to admit to a marble-run addiction. I once sat through an entire birthday party, with the cat of the house, watching marbles roll their way around and around until both the cat and I were hypnotised.

Today it's Sunday and I open the shop by myself. I have only just turned on the coffee machine when I come back from the kitchen to see Darya standing in the shop's interior. My first instinct is to hide, but there's nowhere to go in our tiny shop and already he's smiling at me, and I find myself smiling back despite my fears.

"I thought I'd surprise you. You're always telling me not to visit, but I couldn't wait any longer," he says.

"It's so good to see you." I'm desperate to touch him. "But this is a bad time, I'm busy, sorry."

"Right, loads of customers milling about." He grins at me and looks around the empty shop.

"Not that kind of busy." I point back towards the kitchen. "Cupcakes to be baked and decorated kind of busy."

"Let me watch."

"Not a chance, no way."

"Why not?"

"I'll suffer from performance anxiety if you're there to observe me," I tell him.

"Rubbish! Come on, let me stay."

"You can stay for a fresh cup of coffee and a leftover cupcake.

But you can't stay long." Not long enough to meet Rakel. "I really have to work. Please." I put the closed sign back on the shop's front door and take Darya into the kitchen where the percolated coffee wraps us in its aroma.

He looks out the window and sees a pair of cats grooming each other, tongues over ears, near our dustbin. He pulls a face. "I have a cat phobia. Okay, maybe more of a cat allergy."

"So does my father."

"Wow, I have so much in common with your family. When am I going to meet them?"

My turn to pull a face.

"My father's always busy with his second wife and young family. And my mother lives hours away, up the coast. Her house is right on the beach."

"All the more reason for me to meet her. Let's take a drive out there one day."

"She doesn't really like strangers. My mother prefers living in a narrow world where she can spend lots of time missing my sister. Besides, she's occupied with a trip she's planning. It's her first one away since Amal's disappearance."

"So you're on your own." His look is almost pitying. He moves closer, his fingers interlocking with mine, but I tug them away.

"Not exactly. I have Rakel." His hand moves back, circles my wrist, pulls me towards him, his lips moving over my face, down towards my mouth.

I taste his heart on my tongue, like those fizzy packets of sherbet you and I used to share, Amal, dipping our fingers into the white powder, tracing it on our tongues, feeling the explosions. Somewhere in my heart there's a click, the sound of a door unlatching, the feel of new space. I want this moment to stretch on forever. But that's impossible.

"Not in front of the cupcakes," I say, and push him away to get him a mug for the coffee.

He pulls me back, holds me tight against his chest, and says, "The cupcakes won't mind, they're happier when you're happy," and kisses me again until my lips part. A part of my brain registers the tinkling bell which announces the opening of the shop door. By the time Rakel walks into the kitchen I have my back to the entrance and am pouring three mugs of coffee.

"Hi." I am composed. "This is Darya, he's an artist. I met him the other day at Madame's. Darya, this is Rakel, my partner."

"Hello," he greets Rakel, whose head is swinging gently from my face to Darya's, like a pendulum. "Malak's told me a lot about you."

"Not really, he's exaggerating. We've hardly had much time …" My voice trails off.

"I'm pleased to meet any friend of Malak's. This is nice."

She's going to have so many questions afterwards, but for now I hand her a mug of coffee, milk with three sugars, and then ask Darya how he'd like his, as if I don't know he takes his coffee with milk and half a teaspoon of sugar.

"So you're an artist?" says Rakel. "What do you paint?"

"Mostly seascapes. In fact I'm preparing for a series of lectures on them and I should be getting back to work." He pushes himself away from the oven he's been leaning against.

I exhale.

"Don't be silly," Rakel tells him, "you have to finish your coffee first, and I'll get you a breakfast cupcake."

"Right, Malak did mention something about a stale cupcake earlier."

"Stale cupcake! She was joking. I've got some lovely fresh ones for you and while you're eating you can tell me all about your painting."

I have the sense that I'm drowning as Darya and Rakel begin to chat about art. But at least there's no exchange of personal information, that is, until Darya says something about Rakel and me living together. She frowns. She says, "Well, I suppose you could say that, but technically we're—" We hear the clatter of female heels entering the shop.

When Rakel goes to the front of the shop I tell Darya that he really does have to leave because I've got to work, but he won't go.

By now, Bonny has arrived, so Rakel comes back into the kitchen.

"Are you married?" Rakel asks him, while she pours him a second cup of coffee.

I stare at her.

"No," he says, "are you?"

I don't look up from covering a cupcake in too much icing sugar. Please don't include me in this conversation.

"I was married, three times," she says, "but some days it feels like that happened to someone else. Of course, that's only when I remember. There are days I can't recall much about my life. That's one of the reasons I wanted to do this memoir-writing class. Has Malak told you about it?"

"Yes, briefly." I can feel him glancing at me, but I pretend I'm too busy to return his look.

"And already it has helped me dredge up my lost memories. I've remembered that my first husband was great in bed but barely able to say 'pass the salt' out of it. Dead from TB at twenty-six."

Usually Rakel adds the comment that this was fashionable at the time, but she doesn't say anything about that now. Maybe she's afraid Darya will think she's callous and not joking.

"Husband number two was a dazzling speaker. And a tender man. He was kicked to death by a horse that happened to be trotting by and took an instant dislike to him."

Rakel has told me he was the kind of man who inspired immediate hatred or love, even in animals, it seems.

"Number three," Rakel smiles at Darya, "brought balance and harmony. He drowned on a family picnic while trying to rescue his much younger cousin who had gotten into difficulty while swimming alone. Which just goes to show that no good deed goes unpunished."

Darya seems unsure whether to laugh, or not, and, just then, Bonny comes in to ask Rakel about a price and pauses in the doorway to give Darya the once-over. Rakel pushes her out, although Bonny manages to turn around and look at Darya again.

Now Rakel's gone, I tell Darya he has to leave, he's disrupting our routine. He says he'll go if I show him where we keep the vanilla, but I shove him out the back entrance where he lingers to kiss me before I reluctantly shut the door on him.

Rakel returns to find me whipping butter for icing sugar and when she asks me where Darya is I tell her he had an urgent phone call from a buyer. When did I learn to lie so efficiently? She leaves it at that but, for the rest of the day, whenever I look at her, I find her watching me contemplatively.

That Sunday we're uncharacteristically quiet and Rakel suggests we take the rest of the day off. Bonny and Kwezi vanish together before Rakel has an opportunity to retract her offer. Recently, they went on a date (not sure what happened to Bonnie's boyfriend) and since then they've become inseparable. Now they appear to be cemented to each other's sides. Earlier in the week, they even carried a cup of coffee to Mrs Thomas together, one held the cup, the other the saucer.

When I get home, I find Precious outside on his balcony. He looks happy and tells me he wants me to meet someone, then he leaves. I wait for a minute or two and when he doesn't reappear with his mystery guest I climb over the balcony to his house. Though his home is built along the same lines as ours, it's like entering a parallel universe. After Shireen got over the horror of him moving out, she came in to decorate the place in her own image, in vivid colours with mirrors everywhere.

When you enter his lounge it feels as though you're in the middle of a whirling kaleidoscope. I don't suppose Precious notices.

Today, when I walk in, I see the woman Precious wants me to meet sitting on the blue-and-red flower-patterned couch. There's a vacant look to her gaze that makes her instantly recognisable as one of Precious's girlfriends. Usually, they have the zombie-like stare and Zen-like speech patterns of the drug overindulged. Occasionally, some of them are frenetic, the kind who scour the toilet with your electric toothbrush (when they're not trying to have sex with it). But this one seems particularly vacant, and then, in an instant of recognition, I realise she's not breathing. Precious walks in, grinning like a new father.

He says, "I see you two have met." He seems serious.

"Yes," I tell him. Amal, what else is there to say?

"So, what do you think?"

"Mmm, she's lovely." I reach out and touch her cheek. It's surprisingly soft, and warm. And weird. If she was food, I'd be anorexic.

I had an anorexic friend of sorts, Fiona, during my last weeks of writing exams at school, after your disappearance, Amal. We were connected through our height (both of us were head and shoulders above our classmates), my loss (everyone thought I was mysterious and untouchable after you vanished), and her strangeness (her wrist was the size of other people's middle fingers). She never ate, even though her bones threatened to pierce through her remaining flesh, the way chicken bones do when you're eating a leg. I often imagined I could see right through her.

Once, hurrying between university classes on an October morning, I bumped into her again. She was there with a much older man, checking out possible venues for a photographic shoot. She was living with him, she said, although he had an old white wife in an old white country somewhere. But he was a good career move. She'd become a photographic model.

After that, we stayed in touch, erratically. She'd stop over at Celestial Cupcakes whenever she was in Cape Town (she travelled extensively) and sniff the cakes. Sometimes she'd even sip at a coffee, black, no sugar, no milk, take a small bite out of a plain, vanilla-flavoured cupcake and then excuse herself to use our toilet. She said she had to keep her weight (what weight?) under control because her lover, the photographer, weighed her every morning. He said he'd leave his wife and marry her if she lost a few more kilograms. She was forty-six kilograms the last time I saw her and hadn't had her period in years.

Precious says, "Jalebi's exquisite, isn't she?"

"Right," I say, "well, I'm off. I'll leave you two to get better acquainted."

I make my way back to my side of the balcony and flop down on our soft-as-a-mother's-lap couch, where I find myself indulging in some fantasises of my own, involving a man to whom I'm not married.

Needless to say, I don't see Precious for the rest of the day. Taj is on call, and Darya is preparing for his art classes. So I'm alone for the afternoon. I think of driving over to visit Mum, but I know she's trying to finish off as much of her memory quilt as she can before leaving for Canada. Instead, I decide to do the homework Alice set us. But it's hard to choose what to write about.

The memoir-writing course was Rakel's idea, but it's not as though she had to bully me into joining. She just said, "Malak, I've enrolled us in a memoir-writing course and you'll have to drive me to the classes." Rakel gave up driving after an incident involving a STOP sign a few years ago. So we drive out to the False Bay area, once a month, on a Thursday evening.

Last year, she enrolled us in sewing classes. You won't read about those classes in this memoir, Amal, or how I managed to sew a button to the leg of the pants I was wearing at the time. Nor will you read about the classes in flower arranging or my attempts at candle-making. And I won't bother you with the year we did yoga and I fell asleep every single time during the closing meditation. Rakel said I snored.

So you can imagine I wasn't hopeful about embarking on a writing course. Although when I met Alice and saw her lovely bookshop I softened a little. The books spoke to me; they called out to me like those hookers in Amsterdam that Taj took me to see on our delayed honeymoon. Not that those women actually called to me. They just sat behind their windows and stared back at me, evaluating my potential as a client. They reminded me of the cats I wanted to adopt at the SPCA after you'd gone, after I'd married Taj. Those cats, with their knowing eyes, a stumble away from death. I couldn't choose one, I wanted them all. So I went away with none.

Not that Taj wanted me to choose a hooker. Don't get me wrong, Amal, he only took me there because it was a touristy thing to do, like the bicycles we hired, the museums we visited, the water-spitters we ogled on church spires, the dagga he suggested we smoke in the coffee shop and the visits to the glass-blower and, of course, the cheese-makers. I imagined that since this was the area where Oma was born I might see her ghost wandering the streets, but although I thought I caught the scent of cloves in the air, I didn't find her anywhere.

Even though I read prolifically (a book a day keeps the doctor away – apart from Taj, that is), I never imagined I'd write a book and certainly not a memoir. And I never realised how big and empty a page without words on it can look. I don't suppose I should write about Darya for my homework, but I could also write something about Taj.

There was that day, soon after our first wedding anniversary, when I came home and found Taj weeping into a bottle of whisky, surrounded by photos of you and him. They were the professional ones taken to announce your engagement, the ones where your throat is covered in Oma's diamonds. Do you remember? They were taken at the beach near the hotel you were going to be married at. (Yes, I'm afraid that's where we also had our reception.) Taj dazzles in a blue suit and lemon shirt. He looks like he took fashion advice from Precious that day. Amal, you're wearing a dress in the colours of the sea at dusk. It's pinched in at the waist, showing off the details of your fairy figure, and it has a scooped neckline from which your necklace shines. That dress was once Mum's, and now it's forever part of the remembrance quilt.

Of course I wanted to cry with Taj, but I couldn't. The pool in which my tears swam was frozen over by an impenetrable murky crust that nothing could melt, not love, not the sun, not even sadness. But as I watched his tears through my clear, dry eyes, our love for you bonded us more permanently than the fragile piece of blue paper which declared us husband and wife. You see, because of this love he feels for you, it's possible for me to tolerate and forget all his misdemeanours. Maybe a baby would have allowed me to fall in love with him. But pregnancy never happened.

Instead I had to watch Dad blow a name into the new ear of his unmarked daughter, the first bare duckling. He didn't seem disappointed that it was a girl. By the time his third daughter with his new wife arrived, he wore a stoic expression. I wasn't asked along to watch his fourth and fifth daughters get their names, which may explain why I can never remember them. I know what I'll write for class, Amal. I'll write about you and me, the way we were.

Amal and I are cuddled together in my bed. We've stuck a corner of my pink sheet into the underside of her top bunk, so that we can pretend we're in a tent. Amal's slept in a real tent with Dad. It was brown, she said. Dad's never taken me camping. I'm too small, he says. Even though I'm bigger and taller than Amal is, she's older. I don't understand why, because my birthday's the day before hers. It makes the front of my head sore when I think about it, so I try not to do this a lot. My pink sheet is nicer than a brown tent. Sometimes, if I'm feeling scared, I suck on the edge of the sheet. It tastes warm, like the Sunday when we went on a picnic to the sandy park with only one swing and all the children had to line up for a turn.

Tonight I'm not frightened because the room is dark but not black. I can still see the outline of my white cupboard because the light is on in the passage and it shines into my room. I can hear Mum in the kitchen. She's listening to the radio as she washes the supper dishes.

The other reason I'm not scared tonight is because Oma and Mrs Truffles are visiting. Oma is knitting one of her red-and-purple socks with four knitting needles and Mrs Truffles is washing herself, keeping one blue eye on her fur, which looks just like the colour of my favourite bar of chocolate, and the other on the strand of Oma's fluffy wool as it bounces around while she knits. Mum doesn't like me to talk about Oma or even Mrs Truffles, so when she comes in to give us a goodnight kiss I don't tell her that they're sitting on the edge of the bed, although Mrs Truffles is purring so loudly she sounds like the motorbike of the man who lives across the road and wakes us up far too early every Saturday morning.

I don't understand why Mum can't hear (or even see) Oma. Amal says it's because her ears are old and older people only hear things that interest them. Like Dad can hear the rugby scores on the radio when we're driving in the car, even when there's hooting all around us, but he can't hear Mum tell him to put the rubbish outside although she could be standing right next to him. Mum also can't hear me in the supermarket when I want sweeties, but she can hear Amal crying in her sleep in the middle of the night, and she'll rush into our room and switch on the light, and say "There, there, baby, it's all right, Mum's here."

The one time I mentioned Oma's visit on a day their ears were open, Mum and Dad got strange looks in their eyes and then looked at each other with their lips pulled all funny. Dad got the imam (who always confused me because he was a man but he wore a dress) to visit. The imam burnt fat incense blocks everywhere in the house. They smelt horrible. That night even the food tasted of incense.

When we were alone Amal called me a stupid child and said that if ever I told anyone that Oma was visiting she'd smack me silly. Amal is smaller than me (she still wears her three-year-old clothes although she's five and I'm already wearing seven-year-old clothes although I'm four) but she can pinch really hard and it leaves marks on my skin for a long time afterwards. She also said Oma and Mrs Truffles would never speak to me again. That's as bad as being pinched. I love talking to Oma. I love to hear that what she misses most, being dead, is not being able to eat. I don't want her to go away.

The next day Mum has to wash the curtains in our room because the incense smell got stuck in their folds and made me cough all night, which kept everyone else up too.

That's what I remember, Amal. You probably remember something else. I know that while the exorcism went on, Mum wept.

Perhaps she was hoping it was true that in some dimension her grandmother was still alive. Maybe Mum was just sad that both her daughters were nuts and believed they were being visited by their dead great-granny. Maybe she thought next we'd be seeing her dead parents.

Do you remember how our grandparents died? I can't tell you exactly, and now that I'm an adult I've never asked Mum. I know it had something to do with a drunk driver going through red traffic lights. I know Mum told us about the accident when we were little, and afterwards I used to worry all the time about traffic accidents and drunk people and the speed of life and how accidents seemed to occur randomly all the time. God, Amal, do all children worry about death and dying to this morbid extent? Do you remember how, for years, each time we got into a car, I'd make Dad check for oncoming cars first, before we moved off from a red robot? Of course Dad's always been a cautious driver, especially when driving his "investments".

Mum said that if she thought about her parents' accident all the time then she'd never drive and would we want that? Living where we did it was almost impossible to get anywhere without a car.

I wonder if you remember Oma at all. I wonder if you're with her now.

Without thought I reach for my phone and call Darya.

"Hey," he answers, "I was just about to call you! Do you feel like going for a walk?"

"That's exactly what I feel like doing."

We have a verbal tug of war about who's going to fetch whom, which I win. I can hardly have him come to the house I share with Taj.

On the way over I wonder what I'm doing, driving off to pick up a man when I'm already married. But I forget all about my conscience when I see Darya waiting outside the guesthouse and feel a strange pulse beating in my throat. In the car he suggests we follow the coast road. He says he wants to record the colour of the Atlantic at sunset now that it's almost autumn, and he shows me his fancy camera, tells me that often he paints from the photographs he's taken. He says he should be able to move back home in the next few days and that he'll invite me around to eat. My fingers begin to feel slippery on the steering wheel, lubricated by guilt and maybe something else I'd prefer not to think about.

"If the builders were working on your studio, why did you move out of your house?"

"The noise, I couldn't stand the noise. Besides, they promised they'd be finished in a week and I was dumb enough to believe them. I don't mind. If it wasn't for them we'd never have met. It was nice seeing you this morning in your natural habitat, even if you weren't that happy to see me."

I ignore him and concentrate on the erratic driving of the minibus taxi in front of me.

"So what were you doing before you called me?" he asks.

"I'd finished a writing exercise and was feeling a bit down."

"What did you write about?" He reaches over to caress the back of my neck. "Your sister?"

I nod. The car is almost silent except for the soft chatter of the radio.

"Yes, I wrote something about Amal. Well, I tried to, but I can't write the way some of the women in my class do, providing impeccable detail when they recall conversations they had as children."

He kneads my neck with his knuckles and then his fingers begin to travel lower, as far down as the restriction of my shirt will allow.

I say, "I'm sure Amal and I never used language when she was six and I was five. I can remember colours from our childhood. The smiling yellows of the daises we picked on the vacant plot of land next to our house. The pinks of our identical summer dresses that looked like Smarties. The splashes of red, when we fell, and warm, thin blood trickled out of our knees like leaky taps. The cool blues of early-morning visits to the beach with our mum and dad."

"You remember in colour. There may be an artist trapped inside of you somewhere," he says.

"No, it's not just colour. I remember good things, mostly the happy moments, but not the details, at least not always."

I turn on the car's wiper to brush away flecks of dirt on the windscreen. I say, "I do remember the last words we ever spoke to each other. They're impossible to forget."

We've reached the sea and when I open the car door, he's there, lifting me out, slipping my hand in his and drawing me along behind him. He makes us stop along the way so he can take photos, and even though I've been on this walk too many times to count, today, everything looks different. We walk close to the edge of the quay. Aside from a solitary fisherman surrounded by several hopeful seagulls, we're alone. Darya unpacks his camera and immediately begins clicking away. He turns around to make sure I'm still close.

"Why do you like to paint the sea?" I ask.

Darya says, "I think it's because the sea is all about motion, about journeys, movement." He glances over at me to see if I'm listening. I nod to encourage him.

"So even though the finished painting is immobile, it's captured the movement of the sea and it tells a story about that moment. It's hard to explain." He turns away from the camera to see if I understand.

"No matter how often I do this," his arm indicates both his camera and the sea beyond it, "I'm always captivated by the repetitive movement of the waves breaking on the shore, by the energy of the sea. The sea is a living creature and I want people viewing my paintings to feel that life force." Throughout his speech, he's been glancing over at me, trying to gauge my reaction.

"And the photographs? Do you always paint from photos?" I ask.

"My canvasses are usually quite large and although I've tried to work from studios with sea views I find it better to use a combination of sketches and photos."

He's stopped taking pictures and we've begun to walk along the quay. He takes my hand in his again.

"I paint in layers, and each layer has to dry before I can apply details. It's like a journey. I love it, even when I hate the work and end up binning it."

"I hope that's not after you've been waiting for layers to dry."

"Sometimes it's right at the beginning, sometimes it's near the end."

He stops walking, pulls me towards him and holds me in his embrace. After an instant of self-doubt, I sink into the folds of his shirt – it smells of something flowery that must be fabric softener. Beneath his shirt I can feel his heart beating against my cheek. I can't remember when last I've been held like this, when last I've been hugged with any degree of intimacy and warmth. I want to curl up and fall asleep inside of him, forever. When he tells me to come back to the guesthouse with him I can only nod my agreement.

I've never been inside one of Madame's bedrooms, and as soon as I enter I feel as though I'm suffocating in printed flowers. Roses and their painted petals drip on the duvet cover, violets cluster on a tablecloth, lilies spread themselves across the sofa like damsels in distress and lotuses unfurl on the carpet.

He kisses me and I stop breathing as he pulls me onto the bed. I find my fingers unbuttoning his shirt. As my hands run over his torso, I can feel his heart beating, the taut muscles of his stomach and, below that, what must be an appendix scar. Have I ever taken off Taj's clothes, I wonder, as my hand slips to Darya's zipper. He undresses me. Later, when I get dressed again, each piece of my clothing looks like it belongs to someone else.

Afterwards, long after we've left each other, it feels like he's still there with me, like a new limb.

That night, in bed with Taj, I am mystified by thoughts of men who have multiple wives, or even those who have multiple affairs, like Taj. How on earth do they do it? How do they indulge in circular cross-pollination without guilt? I'm careful not to touch Taj for fear of him wanting sex and taking away some of the magic I felt with Darya. I fall into a restless sleep and find you there, Amal, but you keep swimming away from me. You won't wait for me, and I can't catch up with you, not even in my dreams.

Second Beginnings

This evening I'm clutching Alice's cappuccino to help unfreeze my fingers. The foamy leaf on the surface hasn't disintegrated, although my hands have been wrapped around the cup for several long minutes. We're all of us wearing light jackets or cardigans, and Alice has brought out an electric heater, one bar simmering smokily in the background as it burns away the dust motes floating inside it.

Rakel is talking to Lucy about her recent acquisition, a bonsai plant, and the other women are orbiting the plate of ginger biscuits Alice has placed on a side table. For a change, I've finished my homework (the story about you and me, Amal), although I'm embarrassed to give a copy of it to the other women, as Alice expects us to do. But when Lucy and I exchange pages, she says something that makes me realise she's just as nervous.

Today, Alice is wearing a black scarf wrapped around her throat and when she greets us her voice sounds hoarse. Maybe I should tell her that according to Taj the best way to prevent a cold is to wash your hands regularly. She begins talking and

I strain to hear her until everyone has stopped unzipping bags and slapping pens on the table.

Alice says, "Writing accurate facts is great, but they may not draw your reader into a deeper understanding of the story. You need to combine facts and imagination. For today's writing exercise, I want you to describe a dream, possibly a recurring dream. Show how the dream reality contrasts with your everyday reality." Alice picks up her timer. "You may begin."

I'm not sure, Amal. Can we describe my dreams of you as recurring? Or are they some kind of alternative reality? By the time I'm finished daydreaming about you and doodling another complex volcanic egg, Lucy is volunteering to read hers.

After hours of struggling, of pushing and sweating, of risking eternal damnation by swearing under my breath, of straining my oily body until I'm too tired to care about going to hell, after all that I don't need my mother to tell me that the baby is the wrong colour. I can see it in her eyes, that drip drip drip drippitty-drip like the tap with the broken washer that my husband has still not replaced even though we're in the middle of a drought.

My baby is as blue as my mother's eyes. There were moments during this ordeal when I forgot to breathe, but he has forgotten to live. My mother swaddles him in a warm white towel that turns him indigo and she puts him in my arms. I hear her murmur the love-lullaby of my childhood. I wake up empty.

Alice gently calls us back to our own writing lives.

Celestial Cupcakes is experiencing a boom in April and everyone's favourite is our new cupcake, an angel made of vanilla sponge and caramel sauce. The too-sweet smell of caramel cooking in the shop's kitchen sets my teeth on edge. I'm even beginning to tire of the smell of vanilla too, although Darya adores it. He makes me wear it like perfume on the backs of my knees. I wish he would call, though Rakel would wonder who I'm speaking to. No one calls me, except her.

Did I ever tell you that the day after you disappeared Mum bought herself a cellphone? Then, a few days later, she bought a second phone whose number only Koos knew. She waited for news. She waited for her phones to ring. She waited for the knock on the door. She waited for you to come home, Amal.

Occasionally, her Koos-phone would ring. She'd answer it and take the phone to her bedroom. Afterwards, after that conversation, empty of news, Mum would look, if not happy, then, at least, contained. There would be a lessening in the tightness of her lips, or her brow would clear for a few minutes.

I met Koos soon after my marriage, on a day when both he and I were visiting Mum. Even that early in the morning, the armpits of his shirt were stained. When he lifted up one of Oma's ivory tea cups in fingers that resembled puffy éclairs, I was sure the delicate handles would break. You must remember Oma's favourite tea set, Amal? You know, the one with those brittle-looking cups she said she'd brought with her from Holland on her first trip to Kimberley? She took them with her to India and then to Cape Town when she and Opa returned to

South Africa. From the sound of it, she travelled everywhere with those cups. I imagine they were her surrogate children. Over the years, the teacups have become so fragile that they look like origami. Mum should keep them in a display cabinet and protect our last link to Oma, but she says Oma never believed in keeping things around to look pretty behind glass.

Perhaps I was jealous, but it irritated me that Mum seemed so much more relaxed in Koos's presence than she was in mine. Okay, so they were about the same age, which I suppose gave them a certain communal history, albeit across a broken fence. He was white, with a coloured grandmother, he was quick to inform us. It was a change to hear that: remember, Amal, how people in our community were usually so quick to point out the whiteness of their ancestors?

Once Mum moved nearer to Inspector Koos's base they became closer than ever, and even after he retired he was always popping round to visit her with packets of yucky organic ginger sweets which Mum claimed to be fond of. By then he was no longer Inspector Koos, but he visited Mum if he had any information about you, Amal, or even if he hadn't. Of course Koos could never bring you into Mum's home, just like I can't bring Darya into mine. But at least everyone knows you were once around, Amal, and I can speak about you, whereas, aside from Rakel, no one even knows Darya exists.

And he's not happy about it, especially about not being able to visit me at home. But he doesn't understand and I can't blame him for becoming more than a little frustrated with the fact that he's never even seen where I live. Don't judge me, Amal, you've never had to deal with complications like these. You've never even had to go shopping for groceries.

Actually, I never go shopping for groceries either. Taj does. I think he believes it makes him attractive to other women: he is like the lone wolf, transmogrified into the lone male shopper. Are you wondering why I don't seem to care about his infidelities, Amal? I'm not really sure. Maybe it's because I know I'm not you. And, anyway, it's not as if I can criticise Taj. After all, I'm having an affair now, aren't I?

You know, Darya reminds me of you. Like you, he's with me all the time, a ghost in a shadowy corner of my mind. And, like you, he's more present when he's absent. Not that he's been missing from my life. We've had several dates and many of them have ended in his bed, with our arms and legs entwined.

With Taj, I always know when there's a new lover on the scene. He becomes extra attentive towards me. "Here's a cup of coffee, baby," he'll offer late at night when he gets home, even though, by now, after all these years of marriage, he should know I drink tea in the evenings. Or he'll bring me a gift. A tennis bracelet, or a silk scarf in a flamboyant colour only Shireen would wear. At least he spares me new tricks in bed. Unless that's because he doesn't learn any. It would be nice to be able to speak to Taj about the fact that I'm involved in another sexual relationship. He'd be able to give me advice, wouldn't he? I suspect he'd even be able to make me see things more clearly, to help mop up my tears even if I've never been able to help to erase his grief for you. I know that you and Taj would have been a perfect couple had you married.

Who knows, maybe I'm the sort of person who should never have married. Which is why you'll find my news strange. Darya has proposed. I know this must come as a surprise. It's not as if I've told you much about him. This memoir has turned into a rambling conversation with you, but there are certain things that I find impossible to discuss, even with you, Amal. Sometimes you don't seem real. Sometimes I wonder if I ever knew you or if you've always been a ghost to me, like Oma. Sometimes I think I've invented Darya, if only to make me taste happiness, to knit up my wounds. Our affair has had the quality of a dream, much like one of the dreams you and I share. He's never seemed real. Our entire relationship has felt like playacting, as though I've been breathing underwater, right at the edge of a dream. But his proposal has woken me up. This is real. This is my life.

I can't tell you Darya's precise words, Amal, but here's how I remember it:

We are at his favourite beach. He has surprised me with a picnic lunch that he's prepared himself, and he's even brought a red-and-white checked tablecloth which he lays out right on the edge of the waves.

"Malak," he says. "I know we only met a few weeks ago and that we hardly know each other. Come to think of it, you know more about me than I do about you. Maybe that's what I love about you, that you're a woman of mystery."

My breath halts. Does he mean he loves me or is that an expression?

"But I don't for a single minute think you've entered into this" – his hand swings between the two of us – "lightly." He pauses, seems to be searching for words. "I know it's very soon, and maybe you'll think I'm crazy, but, Malak, the truth is, I want to marry you."

My stomach flips over. He takes hold of my hands in both of his, but I'm afraid to look at him. Amal, is this how you felt when Taj proposed to you?

"Look at me, Malak."

But I can't. I don't want to see his expression.

"Please."

My body feels heavy and all I can hear is the deep silence between us.

"Unless of course I've made a mistake," he says, keeping his voice light. "Maybe you don't love me."

I can't speak. But I can manage a smile which seems to reassure him.

Darya clears a place on the picnic blanket and lies back, pulling me with him so that my head rests on his chest. He picks up an almost closed mussel shell, plays with it between his fingers, and says, "This is for you."

He moves the shell from his fingers to mine. He's prized it open a bit further while he's been playing with it and, when I try to shut it, it pops open again, wider, revealing its contents. Inside there's a fine spattering of beach sand and on top of that a fat pearl ring set in diamonds. I imagine the pearl originally in a shell much like this, extricated from under a living mollusc. I look into his face. He stares back and then turns away. I don't know what to say.

I've only known him a few weeks. How can I marry him? Not forgetting, of course, the small matter of my being married already.

"Is it ethical for a vegetarian to give presents of pearls?"

"Maybe not. It's a moral dilemma we can wrestle with in bed every night of our married lives." He smiles at me. I look away.

I tell him, "Pieces of grit form pearls."

"At this moment, you're very much like one of those irritants," he says, caressing my hair. "Will you answer my question?"

I keep my face lowered, nuzzling his armpit so that I can avoid meeting his eyes. I love him. It's that simple.

"What question?" I ask. "Ask me. Say the words."

I move away from him and sit up.

He doesn't speak. The silence between us is filled by the shrieks of a toddler whose toes have encountered the coldness of waves. Seagulls fly over the child's head in vaguely menacing circles, as if deciding whether or not to whisk the tot away. Maybe that's what happened to you, Amal. Maybe you were kidnapped by a flock of pirate seagulls and even now you're forced to prepare their daily meals of sushi.

"You know what I want," says Darya.

"No, I don't. What exactly do you want?" My next word is stifled as he pulls me back towards him, and pushes me deeply into the blanket, until I feel the sand's supportive warmth through the fabric of my T-shirt. Above me, Darya shifts his upper body, crushing me into the weight of the moment and the reality of his existence. He wraps his right leg around my left and looks into my face until I see myself in his eyes. He bends closer, kisses the corner of my mouth and sucks my bottom lip lightly, pulling it in between his fuller lips. His tongue tastes mine momentarily before releasing it.

"So?"

He puts his arm under my neck, pillowing the back of my head, lifting me closer to his face, drawing my gaze into his. The skin of his usually taut cheeks appears to be dissolving the way butter softens when you're creaming it with brown sugar.

"I'll have to think about it."

Well, Amal, what else could I say? Of course I can't marry him, but how can I tell him that? I know what it's like to live with a broken heart.

"Okay, as long as you don't think the word 'no', please. And a 'yes' means I'd like to do it really soon, before I leave. No pressure," he teases. "Here, while you're thinking, keep the ring as a talisman. My dad gave it to my mother when they got married."

Oh, the story of my life, another second-hand ring. He slips the ring onto my finger as though we're already committed to each other. My knuckle halts the journey for a heart-stopping breath, but then softens a little so the ring can slide home to rest at the base of my finger. "Malak, I'm sorry you're not agreeing to marry me right now. Don't make me wait too long."

The drive home is a long, silent one, although, occasionally, I hear the click of knitting needles from the backseat.

That evening, when I get home, Taj is out and there's a note on the fridge reminding me that we're having supper the next night with one of his more fecund patients, who has recently had her fifth baby. I'm relieved at his absence. But, Amal, I wish you were here right now so I could see the look on your face and hear your laughter. Later, after I've made myself a sandwich and am deciding whether it's worth getting up from the sofa, where I've been attempting to sleep, Precious stumbles over the balcony for a late-night chat. I'm glad to see him. At least he will distract me from the thoughts that are tumbling about in my head like drunken acrobats. Tonight, Jalebi is conspicuously absent – since he got her he's dragged her along to every visit. Maybe he's bored with dressing and undressing her, all that maintenance, like having a baby. Precious sinks into the sofa across from my mine, and one look at him tells me he's been indulging in something besides Jalebi. Actually, a slightly stoned Precious is exactly what I need right now. In this mood, Precious can wax lyrical on any subject. All he needs is a prompt.

"Hey, Precious, did you hear that your cousin Mo is taking a second wife? What do you think about plural marriages?"

He takes the bait. "Well," he says, leaning his head back against the chair, "according to modern Islamic feminist interpretations ..." And he's off.

Amal, I think I told you that Precious has been doing a postgraduate degree in something vaguely religious for several years, so he does actually know what he's talking about. But it still irritates me that a man with a sex-doll should be allowed to say the word *feminist*.

I tune back in to Precious in time to hear him say, "… this means that women in Islam, at least in the past, in previous centuries, enjoyed the kind of legal status that women in other cultures were deprived of at the time. Islam was considered a radical religion because of its recognition of women's rights. But …" He reaches into the pocket of the jacket he's wearing and takes out a small silver flask, examines it, then slips it back into his pocket. "Can I have some mint tea?" he asks.

Mum's introduced Precious to her range of organic tea.

"Okay, come with me while I make it." He follows me into the kitchen, where he sways in the doorway while I fill the kettle with water.

"So, you were saying?"

Precious looks at me blankly for a second or two before his eyes light up again.

"Right," he says, "so over the centuries something's been lost because of the way some men interpreted Qur'anic scripture to suit themselves. The Qur'an is for all Muslims, women and men are equal in the eyes of Allah. Like, women are people too. They have the right to divorce, to inherit, and to study, 'from the cradle to the grave'. Or something like that."

I stuff a tea bag into each of our cups (none of that fancy

teapot stuff Mum indulges in) and pour water over the bags. So is Jalebi an equal too? I wonder. But then, of course, Precious will tell me she's not real.

He says, "As an example, for years, Muslim women weren't told that they could keep their surnames when they got married, that they could contract their marriages *and* divorces, and that they could inherit and choose who to leave their money to. They were kept ignorant of the truth of polygyny and purdah."

What he is saying is interesting, and for a moment I forget how idiotic Precious can be.

"Tell me something about sex," I order him, "sex and Islam." I pick up both cups and gesture with my head towards the lounge.

I hear him stumble behind me, saying, "Islam is very accepting of sex."

"Right, just as long as you're married. Or you're a man having sex with one of your wives."

"That's not true."

"No?"

"Yes. No. You're confusing me." I hand him his teacup and he slithers deeper into the couch.

"Let me tell you," he says, "that's another male-created myth, like the one about a woman having to wear a scarf all the time. The Qur'an says that both men and women have to dress modestly. Only one verse actually refers to women wearing veils – the one that says the Prophet's wives should be behind a hijab when they were talking to men."

"So what are you trying to tell me? That the scarf thing only applies to the Prophet's dead wives?"

"The jury's out on that one. What's more important than covering a few strands of hair is modest dressing. For men and for women. Like, if you're wearing lots of clinking jewellery that draws attention to yourself, that's not modest dressing."

"So, then, why did you get all those glass bangles for Jalebi?"

"Is this what these questions are about, me and Jalebi? You're so judgemental. Sex is a foretaste of paradise."

"Even when it's with a doll?"

He ignores me and sips at his tea until I remember I have a cup in my hand too. He drinks the rest of his tea and puts his cup on the little table standing between us. Then he places a hand in front of his eyes. He appears to be counting his fingers. When he reaches a number that seems to satisfy him, he starts to speak again.

"Islam doesn't think sex is immoral, unlike Christianity where sex is considered a kind of sin or something evil and corrupt that you have to defeat."

"Right, so what you're saying is that Islam doesn't see sex as evil, only women."

"What are you talking about? You're not listening. You're twisting my words. That's not true. That's not what I said."

"Of course it is.

I suddenly feel angry, Amal, with Precious, with Taj, even with Darya. I'm not sure why. Precious continues, "Listen, you have to understand that the current patriarchal interpretation of Islam is not necessarily authentic, *original* Islam. I've told you before, it's about male-interpretation. The Qur'an doesn't encourage people to view sex as self-gratification."

"You screw a doll, isn't that about self-gratification?"

He doesn't answer me. Instead he says, "You have to think of the pleasure and happiness of your partner as well. In Islam, women aren't expected to lie back and think of England."

"So, what you're saying is that women can be in control of their sexuality in bed, with the single husband they're allowed, even though he can be a much-married man? Just as long as they know they don't have any rights outside of the bed."

"That's a myth too."

"What is?"

"Multiple marriages."

I raise my brow at him in a poor imitation of Rakel and put down my cold tea on the table near his cup.

"Multiple marriages aren't allowed?"

"Listen, Malak, you must understand that the Prophet lived during an age of war, when there were many many destitute widows and orphans – polygyny at the time was like an act of charity."

I snort in a marvellous imitation of a pig, if I say so myself, Amal. Do you remember our animal impersonations? Your frog was spectacular.

"At that time, a second marriage wasn't about finding a sexy trophy wife. Then it was about making the best of harsh and depressing circumstances. It was a way of offering women pro-tection, even if that sounds crazy now."

He bends forward to peer into his empty teacup as if the words he wants are hiding in there.

He says, "The Qur'an is clear that a man's wives have to be treated equally on every possible level. You have to be fair, you have to share love, respect, time, support – but what mere man can do that? And if you can't be fair to your wives, then you shouldn't have more than one wife. The Qur'an doesn't suggest that you can take another wife, or two, or more, just because you're rich or horny or because your first wife can't have kids."

"So, if I'm to believe you, a man who sleeps with silicone, the Qur'an's conditions makes multiple marriages virtually impossible?"

"Exactly. And not even the Prophet could follow the rules. By all accounts, he had a favourite wife."

"Okay, so what about polyandry?"

"Definitely not allowed. Although it was part of pre-Islamic Arabia."

"Really?"

"Yes."

"So these days only men can have loads of spouses?"

"I've told you that's not exactly true. I mean, think about it. Do you agree that Allah is good and fair?"

I shrug. Shrugging is the new habit I've learnt from Kwezi and Bonny. That and the word *whatever*, which can be used to answer any question. For instance: "Why the hell did you give them the bear cupcakes when they ordered giraffes?" Answer: "Whatever." Accompanied by a shrug.

He says, "Since the Qur'an is Allah's word – the word of the just – then how can anything in the Qur'an advocate gender inequality? Think of all the amazing women the Qur'an describes who played important roles in Islam, in the Prophet's life. You'll see this if you focus on the teachings of the Qur'an itself and not patriarchal interpretations."

"Hmm, so men and women are equal, according to the Qur'an?"

"Yes."

"And supposedly equal in our Constitution?"

"Yes."

"Then it seems to me that if polygamous marriages are recognised by our courts, under our equal rights legislation, then polyandry should be legal too." That would certainly make my life easy, wouldn't it, Amal?

Precious is pretending to smoke a pencil he's found on the coffee table near my abandoned journal.

"Precious?"

"Hmm?" The conversation appears to have exhausted him.

"Are there computer records kept of Muslim marriages, here, in the city, or in the rest of the country?"

"No, not as far as I know."

"So there isn't a computer database?"

"No."

"So how are records kept?"

"Manually. In various registers. Marriage officers are supposed to keep records."

"So, if you were married at a different mosque or by a different official and didn't admit to a previous marriage, no one would know you were lying, unless they physically scoured every single existing marriage register in the country?"

"Yes, correct. Which would be extremely difficult, if not impossible, unless you knew exactly what you were looking for."

"So that means that if someone wanted to, they could get married several times to different partners all around the country, or even the province, without anyone knowing?"

"I suppose so."

Which means that if I were to marry Darya … But, no, Amal, I can't even finish that thought.

Precious says, "And it's been done. There are men who get married in secret without their first or second wives knowing. Except, of course, a man needs two witnesses every time he gets married."

"Two men, right?"

"Yes."

"Do they have to be Muslim? The witnesses."

"No."

"Do they have to be known to him?"

"No."

"And the woman? The bride. She needs two witnesses as well, right?"

"Yes."

"Relatives?"

"No," Precious says tiredly, "any males she's given authorisation to represent her. Usually her father, I suppose, and he gets the imam to officiate at the ceremony."

"Okay, so seeing as there are no computer records kept, someone who is married by Muslim rites can marry a different partner legally without the authorities being aware of this?"

"Yes. Why this sudden interest in Muslim marriages?"

"No particular reason, just curious. Thank you, Precious. You've been helpful."

But Precious doesn't hear me. He's fallen asleep with his eyes slightly open, like a tired Jalebi.

The next day, after a sleepless night and even though I'm busy at Celestial Cupcakes, Darya is never far from my thoughts. I know that I have to refuse his proposal. But I don't know how to tell him no, or what to tell him. He doesn't call me or even send a text. He's waiting for my answer.

So I concentrate on my orders: several dozen cupcakes which I still have to shape into caterpillars for a kid's birthday party, four dozen white-and-brown snail cupcakes for another child and, of course, those guardian angels, always in demand, but never there when you need them.

That night, I tell Taj I have a migraine, for the first time in my life (can't use period pains with a gynae husband), and I escape the dinner with the fertility princess. Sadly, this means I'm at home to answer the phone when Shireen calls. We go through the polite motions and I explain that Taj is out. She says I must get him to call her as soon as possible because she believes her heart is weakening. After several minutes of listening to Shireen complain about beggars at traffic lights and how they'd soon be breaking the bones of their children to turn them into career beggars the way they do in India, I really do have a headache. Then she stops herself. She usually tries to avoid mentioning children in my presence. She draws a halt to the conversation, reminds me to tell Taj she called.

I seek refuge from the mutterings in my head in the pile of books on the floor next to my side of the bed. I know that some women buy clothes or shoes and keep them a secret from their partners, but I have a different addiction. I fall into the category of "Hello, my name's Malak, and I'm a book-a-holic." I've been stealthily sneaking books into this house for so long that Taj doesn't know if they're new or not. I take the prices off, which is weird, because it's not like I use Taj's money to buy them. Sometimes, I bring them home without the shop's packets, unclothed like newborns, so Taj remains ignorant of their freshness. I don't know why I'm ashamed of my habit, it's not as if they're drugs, or as though buying books is an illegal activity. The problem is that at any one time I have at least nineteen unread books, waiting patiently on the floor. But I like having them there, it's such a comfort. If my reserve grows low, I panic. Occasionally, Taj, stumbling over a pile of books to get to the bathroom, will tell me it's time to get rid of them, but how do you choose between your children?

Do you remember that gruesome book about a female serial killer, the one we read in our early teens, Amal? We were so terrified, we read it together, me turning the pages, you reading the words aloud. At night, we'd leave it in Mum and Dad's room, because we were so afraid the characters in the book would materialise and spirit us away. But even though it terrified us we still had to finish reading it. We needed to be sure that the serial killer was caught and imprisoned, that he got his just desserts. Of course we were both stunned when the murderer turned out to be a woman. That's the only book I remember happily parting with – I donated it to the local library when I was packing up to move in with Taj.

Yet, I don't cling to any other possessions. I'm ruthless about not accumulating junk, unlike Taj, who still has all his primary school reports. He never throws anything away. Sometimes it drives me crazy, especially with the limited space we have in our townhouse. It's the reason he still has a room in Shireen's house, with his junk in it, and another in Precious's house, with his medical books from his undergraduate years, which by now are either outdated or have their information freely available on the Internet.

But Taj isn't as bad as one of his aunts who, when she died, had a backyard and kitchen filled with hundreds of boxes of unopened cans of food that had long since passed their sell-by date. There were also unused, ancient household electrical appliances. And unopened cutlery sets. There were crates upon crates (piled high, obscuring the sun) of empty cooldrink bottles. The kind that hadn't been manufactured in decades.

There are times when I feel sorry for Taj, but I miss Darya.

Although, sometimes, when I'm with him, I feel as inarticulate as a rock, possibly because of my well-developed conscience. What do you think, Amal? Sometimes I wish I'd been vaccinated against him before we'd ever met, that I'd received some magical drug to make me immune to his charms. What is he to me? A bump in the road of my life that I should drive over and forget about? But I can't forget him, not when he's exerting a pull on me as strong as gravity.

Rakel says I'm behaving differently, that I'm not present. She says she's worried about me, that I should get help. I tell her it's nothing, that it's the memoir-writing course which is absorbing me and making me remember some long-forgotten things. I can't tell her about Darya, that he's haunting me. Sometimes I think I want my love back from him. Or at the very least I want it defined, labelled and stored in a glass jar in a lab where someone clever and competent can analyse it and give me the antidote.

Why couldn't this be a regular tawdry affair, the kind Taj indulges in? Why did I have to meet him? I know you can't help me, Amal, but it feels good writing to you about it. I go to bed with two of my book-security blankets. They put me to sleep as wonderfully as an anaesthetic.

The next morning I shuffle to the kitchen, check for imaginary insects, then drag myself and my coffee to the balcony. The wind makes my eyes water. I reach into the left cup of my bra (yes, Amal, I still sleep in a bra) for my cellphone. I've taken to storing it there ever since I gave Darya my number. I keep it on vibrate because I don't want Taj, when he's around, to see how popular I've become.

I begin to type out a message. I have to let Darya know that I can't marry him. I'd like to tell him the truth, only I'm afraid of his reaction. But instead, I find myself typing out a single word: *yes*. Then I change the small letter *y* to a capital *Y*. I add a full stop. I delete the full stop and add an exclamation mark. Then three more. Finally I settle for a simple *Yes*. Almost immediately the phone vibrates back:

– Yes????????
– Yes.
– I love you!
– I love you.
– When can I see you?
– Getting ready for work, call you soon, xxx.

I switch off the phone before he sends any more texts and before he can call. I'm getting married. Don't tell my husband.

Weren't we told in madressa that getting married fulfils half our duties as Muslims? So surely marrying two men would mean satisfying one hundred per cent of my obligations? There's a mathematical sensibility to that illogical idea that I find comforting. What am I thinking?

I'm on a road with soft, secret hills, hidden valleys. I'm driving the wrong way, with my seatbelt unbuckled, my eyes shut. Of course I can't marry him.

Reader, I married him. Okay, I've wanted to write that for a long time now, Amal. On the day I married Darya, I often thought of Mr Rochester. Although how can I be a bigamist when the country of my birth doesn't recognise my marriage to Taj as a legal contract? Taj and I may as well have got the full moon to officiate at our ceremony as far as our government is concerned.

Mum has flown off to Canada and left me the key to her house. Next week, Taj is off for a conference in a city whose name doesn't have any vowels. Perhaps the universe is conspiring, along with me. Even Precious is absorbed with Jalebi and a university assignment. I tell Rakel I need some time off from my life, that I'm going to stay at Mum's for a while. Simple. And true. She seems pleased that I'm finally taking a break.

What isn't as simple is meeting Darya's family for the first time. Why couldn't he have been an orphan (Cousin Zuhra's favourite kind of man), or at the very least estranged from his family?

By the time we get to his parental home (I pick him up again), my nose is shiny with guilty perspiration and most of my make-up has been wiped away because of the several shirts that I've whipped on and off again. I've settled for jeans (it's what the son of the house wears all the time) and a black shirt which doesn't make me look as though I'm trying too hard. Of course I'm wearing his ring. It helps that I hardly ever wear Taj's rings, so there's no telltale line of pale skin to disguise. Taj has never asked me why I don't wear his rings. I don't think he notices.

Darya's sister, Jay-Jay, opens the door. She's wearing the

same thing as me – dark blue denim and a black long-sleeved shirt. (Thank you, gods, all that huffing and puffing in and out of clothes has paid off.) She's a lot shorter than me and I hope for her sake she's still growing. She sticks out her hand and smiles at me, introduces herself, drags me over the threshold and doesn't stop talking. And that's the way it is with the rest of the family too. It's like I'm an insider because Darya's brought me home. I've felt less at ease at one of Taj's family get-togethers, and they've known me for most of my life. (Maybe that's why.) Darya's mother and stepfather (although no one says 'step') hold hands throughout our visit. She looks like a feminine version of Darya.

For supper, his mother has cooked a traditional breyani (without the meat, because her son says he won't make a cemetery of his body) and it's the best food I've tasted since Mum gave up cooking big meals. I've brought dessert. Cupcakes of course. A few simple ones and a few show-off ones too.

Later, after the dishes have been packed in the dishwasher, his mother leads me to her mauve-and-pink bedroom and presents me with the earrings and necklace that match my engagement ring – they're part of the set Darya's dad gave her when they got married. For my dowry, she gives me some old gold coins that, again, were courtesy of Darya's biological dad. So, Amal, this is how it feels to be a fraud. His mother likes me, and his sister confides school stories while we make tea to go with the cupcakes, by which time I feel like a thief running off with the family jewels.

Of course the whole family wants to be present at the wedding, and arrangements are made to have it in their house. By now I'm squirming. I'm worried that they'll think we're having a hasty marriage because I'm pregnant. I want to reassure them that there's no chance of me adding to the family, but how do I explain that I know I'm infertile because I'm married to a fertility expert?

Darya convinces them not to invite the extended clan, just a small wedding with immediate family. I tell them about you, Amal. At least I don't lie about that. I tell them Mum's away. Another not-lie. They don't pry. They're either very polite, or Darya has told them that I like my privacy. I give them the impression that Dad and I have been estranged since the divorce, and that I'd rather not talk about it. His father arranges the rest. The imam and his entourage will make up the required witnesses.

On the drive home Darya explains that he's committed to a semester at the college, and that he understands I won't be able to come with him at such short notice, that I have my business to think of, but that he expects me to visit. He also suggests that I move into his home, but I tell him that Rakel needs time to adjust to my marriage and my leaving and that I'd rather not be alone. The lies make the soles of my feet sweat, Amal.

I can't believe I'm doing this. I can't believe I'm being this deceitful. Darya's teaching assignment is giving me a reprieve, but when he comes back he'll expect me to live with him and I'll have to leave Taj. Or give up Darya. Any suggestions, Amal?

The rest of the week passes in a blur. I can't tell you what kind of cupcakes I baked, or what food I ate, Amal, or even what I said to those around me. Mostly I'm filled with dread so that I can't sit still, and when I do my left leg jiggles itself constantly. At one point, I tell Darya that perhaps we should wait until after he returns from England so that Mum is also here for the wedding. But he says no, that he's afraid I'll find someone else while he's away. I can hardly mention that I already have someone else.

I wasn't present (literally or figuratively) for my marriage to Taj: Dad just went along to the local mosque, while I and my brittle body sat mummified in ethereal nebulous cloths, with tiers of scarves swathing my hair, my eyes shut but my face left open to the gaze of those keeping vigil with me. It was Dad who must have said the words of acceptance, and when he came back I was a married woman.

But when Darya and I get married, a mere week later, I am in attendance, dressed a lot more simply in black pants, cotton shirt and hand-painted silk scarf, a gift from my Darya. This time my eyes are open, my gaze on Darya. He's still in jeans, I notice, but his mother assures me, in that embarrassed tone mothers sometimes use, that they're new. Although, in the wedding spirit, he seems to be wearing formal shoes instead of his usual tackies or slip-slops. And a new, if unironed, white shirt. Perhaps it's the gleaming shirt that makes the other people in the room seem hazy and insubstantial.

I wonder if I've unknowingly eaten one of Precious's dagga

cookies. Or maybe it's got something to do with my sensitivity to incense, as there's plenty of that on offer today. My throat's beginning to close up. Not a moment too soon I hear the heavy clink of coins, my dowry being exchanged. And it is mine, mine to hold onto, my security. I wonder what Taj gave me as security against our divorce, his death. And where is it? I don't think anyone asked me what I wanted. Yes, I know those were dark days for me, but I can't remember. Maybe Mum knows.

Afterwards we eat. Although we're a tiny group of people, Darya's mother has cooked enough to feed several dozen guests. There's the traditional array of samoosas and bhujias with dhania-layered dips, but there are also mini-quiches and pizzas and freshly squeezed fruit juices and, of course, sweet-meats. When I bite into a gooey piece of jalebi, I experience a cannibalistic flash, but that moment (the guilty instant filled with memories of my other life, my other husband) passes as the sweetness hits my tongue.

All too soon it's time to leave for Mum's house, our honey-moon destination. Darya and I have six days together before he goes away to begin his new job. I've told him that it's imposs-ible for me to join him in England because Rakel won't cope on her own, but that I'll visit as soon as I can, once he's settled in and I've had time to find someone to stand in for me. And six months will go quickly, I tell him. I think to myself: when he's gone I'll be able to think clearly, and imagine a future. Or the end of my future.

The first night as a married couple, after we've made love,

he holds me in his arms, curled like a comma against him, and says, "Malak, I'm going to miss you, I love you."

I already miss him. I don't mention that he's the warm sunny spot in my mind that I go to when the rest of the world is dark and heavy. I don't mention that he's my favourite husband.

Learning How to Leave

The sunset has the look of a bleached lemon, withering on its branch. I can hardly discern the colours of the waves from Alice's window. The darker evenings seem to be affecting not only me, but also the other women in the class. Everyone is subdued.

Alice says, "Today your task is to write about a moment in your life when you negotiated your way over a threshold, or crossed a border." She sets up her egg timer, and we begin scribbling. This time I abandon my doodles and try to write about the dream I had about you last night.

We were travelling in a water-taxi, but there were so many houses around us I thought we might be on our way to visit Darya in the canal-bound area where he's living now. But then I noticed the boat had a flat bottom and a metal decoration on the bow, and when I turned around I saw the single oar, held in the hands of the gondolier. I was glad he wasn't one of those singing ones, but even so I erased him from the dream. It's good to know I have some control over my dream world.

You sat on my left. You said, *Do you know gondolas are built using eight different types of wood?* Your right hand was wrapped around mine, but your left fingers were trailing in the water. Then you brought your hand up out of the water and showed me your fingers, which were coloured crayon-blue. We were adrift in a block of cerulean sea. A sign materialised, warning us of a speed bump ahead. We glided over this, and then with a small smack found ourselves in jade waters, smooth as a fluid necklace.

I turned to you and you showed me wiggling green fingers. The next speed bump gave way to sunflower-yellow water. I stood up – our boat rocked slightly – and looked at the colourful chunks of sea surrounding us. Surely this was the kind of seascape Darya-the-child would have painted. Now your fingers looked like they were covered in egg yolk. You agreed. You licked them, giggling. I'd forgotten the sound of your laughter, the way you breathed out all your chortles before gasping for air. I'd forgotten how much I'd missed the sound. Then we were in orange waters. You said, *A bit of the sun has fallen from the sky,* and you giggled again. But when I slipped my hand into the water, my fingers came up red, smelling of uncooked meat. I woke up.

When Alice asks someone to read, it's Monica who puts up her hand with care, as if it hurts. During one of our earlier classes, Monica regaled everyone with tales of her travels. It made me a little envious, but I know I could never be as adventurous as her. Now she begins to read.

One day when I'm looking for my birth certificate, I find my long-out-of-date, first adult passport. The woman in the photo is unrecognisable with her long hair in corkscrew permed curls and her shiny pinky-purple lipstick. I smile at her. When I open the little book, the pages stick together. I remember our last jarring flight together and the Coke spill. Inside the stained pages there are stamps and dates of entry and exit, evidence of borders crossed and recrossed. Some of these places I only know I visited because of these inky blotches. Of course there are travel articles that I must have written about them, which must be published somewhere.

Here's the stamp for the tiny island with an unpronounceable name whose beach waters were as warm and seductive as a bath at the end of a rainy working day. This must be the place where I ate fish, caught, then cooked, still wriggling, on hot coals. This date I recognise as my arrival in a snowy town, the same time my mother gave up her argument with cancer. Not that I knew it then, in those pre-Internet, pre-cellphone days: no news crossed my doorstep as I walked into the fifth ski resort in seven days. When I returned from the cold they told me Mama had died last week. I wished then that I could revisit a different year, when my mother was young, but once you've crossed a line on the map of your life, there's no going back.

May is another busy month at Celestial Cupcakes: the dreaded Mother's Day. Of course this year it needn't concern me as I am no one's mother, and my own is in Winnipeg, which she tells me has a Muslim population of around one per cent. This bit of census information seems to fulfil her. But it must be Sara and the trips she's arranged for Mum that bring the new lightness I hear in her voice. Or perhaps it's the distortions of the international phone line. All I know is that when Mum speaks to me she sounds like a balloon set free.

It seems that between Darya and Mum I'm always reaching for the phone and doing time-zone calculations in my head. Darya and I don't talk on the phone as much as I'd like, and that's mostly because of my lack of privacy. At work, someone always seems to be around when he calls. At home, I hardly ever seem to have solitude anymore. Precious, when he isn't indulging in Jalebi, has taken to hanging around me all the time, looking mournful.

Even Taj is at home more regularly these days, since he got back from his last trip. Recently, Taj and Precious have started going to gym together. They've taken up yoga. Sadly, not at a convenient time for me to speak to Darya. Perhaps the gym will become Taj's new hunting ground. Amal, do you think Taj feels guilty about sleeping around? He's never seemed awkward around me. Or am I guilt-ridden because of my emotional connection to Darya, the kind of bond that Taj and I, even after all these years, can never share?

The truth is I find it easier to write to Darya. Not only because no one can overhear us, but also because I've begun to enjoy putting words on paper. Or, in this case, on the screen of my flea-sized piece of technology. Although I miss him deeply, cuttingly (the way I miss you, Amal), I like that he's away, that I can keep him contained, boxed, labelled in my tiny techno-toy. It keeps me safe. If he could just stay in my message box, I'm sure he'd spare me a great deal of confusion.

— You sounded down when you called from the airport, like something was wrong.
— No, I was missing you, that's all. Why didn't you come to the airport to see me off?
— I told you I wouldn't do it, you know I hate goodbyes.
— Oh.
— Don't say Oh like that! The winter's going to be bad enough without a Darya cold front.
— So come visit me. It's spring here, you'll be warm. I'll keep you warm.

I wish it were that easy. I wish I could visit and stay with him forever.

I miss him, but since his departure we've been writing to each other several times a day and I like the different dimension that distance has brought us in the form of these messages that fly between us. I feel less tongue-tied when I write to him. I love the anticipation of reading his replies. I even love watching that tiny virtual pen erase words he decides not to send.

There are times when I can't appreciate or dwell on his responses, if he's written and I'm in the middle of work, or Precious is hovering nearby. So on nights when I'm alone I become a word-miser, gathering and studying Darya's syllables.

When we don't communicate, no phone calls, no texting, nothing tangible, I think of him at the oddest moments (even in bed with Taj, especially in bed with Taj), I find Darya's name on my tongue, a memory of him lurking behind my closed eyelids. But, of course, it's not enough for me. I want to taste him. I want to slip under his skin like it's a freshly laundered sheet. I want to see the trickles of sweat at his temples when he climaxes.

At work I take Darya with me, from mixing bowl to oven, from icing sugar and fresh cream fillings to sales (Bonny called in sick), his presence pursuing me silently, invading my head, my body. I line the cupcake trays with anti-sticking spray and his name, whip the fresh cream and chocolate together into mousse and see his face in the glossy finish of the mixture. I smell his cologne in the mint and orange of a special batch of Mother's Day cupcakes. I'm sick of it. I'm homesick for him.

All day I look forward to the evening, when I can write to him. Sometimes it's impossible to wait that long, and I find myself reaching for my phone, texting him, waiting for the invasive beep-beep of his response. Or worse, the silence of his not responding, because he's busy with work, with students, with art, with stupid seascapes. Sometimes I want to exorcise him from my head and heart. He makes me feel like glass: I would be in shards if he were to leave my life.

I love his words even when they don't make sense, Amal. I've got it bad. I've begun to write to him without thinking about what I'm going to write; it's become an unconscious act, like breathing. Maybe it's because most of our communication is through Instant Messaging – it's easier to write without planning.

- Today was difficult. I thought you were probably working hard, too busy to call, so I waited for you to make contact. Then you write two words, okay, four, if you count the subject line. Reminds me of something I read years ago, about erotic stories for men and women. For women there was a lengthy tale, heavy on the adjectives, lots of sensual detail and with a slow, long build-up, but for the male readers, a short single sentence, something about two blondes kissing.
- Maybe I can't express myself as well as you do. I miss you, but I can't find the words to describe my feelings. Help me.
- I can't give you the words. I don't know them. Sometimes it feels as though I barely know you.
- I know who you are. I want you around all the time, please come visit me.
- If I come over, I may never want to come back. This is my life here. You'll swallow me up into yours.
- It's not like we'll live here forever. Come over for a while.

What is he to me? A basic necessity. Food, water, shelter, Darya? How did I ever imagine that Darya, even a faraway Darya, would be easy to evade? How could I have been so stupid not to realise that once we were married he would expect far more from me?

- Malak, why are you scared? Don't you trust me?
- I do, but it's all those nubile students of yours that worry me.

- I'm way too busy to even notice those kids.
- What are you busy with?
- When I'm not teaching I'm painting. You know how you often talk about your sister?
- Yes.
- It's given me an idea for a piece. Memory and childhood. And of course the sea has to be in there somewhere.
- How are you going to do that?
- I'm not sure yet. I'm working on it. The point is that between my painting and you, I don't have time to flirt with students.
- Good, I'm glad. And don't forget to tell them you're married.

Sometimes I hit the Send button, and I think, did I really use those words? I should learn to take each word in hand, to weigh every one of them carefully, like delicate plums, check them for discolouration and worms, polish them to a high gloss before I deliver them.

- Of course you're part of my world! It's just that for now we're mainly connected through the words we offer each other in these notes. Sometimes I like you far away but I also want you close enough to kiss.
- Malak, you know the only way for us to get close enough to kiss again is for you to come visit me.

Last night, Kwezi and Bonny had sex with each other for the first time. I know this because she told me as soon as she came into work this morning. There I was minding my own business, piping peppermint cream onto a chocolate cupcake. Of course a few months ago I wouldn't have cared. But now I listen to Bonny, and the phrases she uses – "It felt like my heart had stopped" – make me realise that Bonny and I aren't all that different.

– You might be entertained, Darya, to know you were the second person to mention their need for a dua from me today. A distant relative called me looking for my mother and then told me to make dua because her husband's in hospital. But in the next breath she said she hasn't slept as well in years, thanks to his absence from the matrimonial bed. I couldn't understand what I was supposed to pray for – that her husband's stay in hospital be prolonged so she can continue to sleep well, or for his speedy recovery? I remember when we were teenagers, my parents would take me and my sister to visit a particular old relative (I'm not sure if she was Mum's or Dad's or if they shared her) who'd always give us money and tell us to make a dua for her. We'd accept the cash and Amal would say we were prayer prostitutes.

Kwezi and Bonny are facing a crisis in their relationship, already. For some reason best know to him, Kwezi wants to meet her family, but Bonny doesn't want him to meet them.

"You're ashamed of me," he says.

"No, I'm ashamed of my family. You don't understand. My family's not like me. And maybe *I'm* not even like me, like the me you know, when I'm with them. My granny's going to tell you how in her day the only darkies (and she'll think she's being polite when she says darkies) were the ones who brought you your milk in glass bottles with silver caps every morning. How can I expose you to that?"

"I don't mind. I'm prepared for that. It's okay, my father won't even allow me to bring a woman home unless there's a string of cows behind her."

"It's a herd of cows," I tell them.

They give me dirty looks. Someone should remind them I'm the boss.

— Malak, I've never asked you: do you want babies one day?
— It's not as though we've had time for serious talks what with you busy sweeping me off my feet.
— Did I?
— You know you did.

No sign of Kwezi or Bonny today. They're not even answering their cellphones, which means that Rakel is selling cupcakes in the front and I'm baking up a storm in the back. This is really getting on my nerves. Rakel says she might fire them, but I doubt she will. She's far too soft with them. Luckily, we're not too busy today. Mother's Day is over, and there aren't that many birthday orders, only a few office functions in the area. In fact, I'm enjoying their absence. No more lovey-dovey looks across the cupcakes.

Mum hasn't been in touch recently. Last time I heard from her was when she emailed to say they were going on a trip to Sara's holiday house near a lake. Maybe they don't have Internet coverage. Perhaps, Amal, Mum just needs a break from remembering I'm alive and you're not.

– You never answered my question.
– What question?
– Do you want a baby?
– Yes, I do.

Bonny loves Kwezi. Decorated in chocolate icing over three cupcakes. How dare they waste my cupcakes? And icing. Just because they're happy. It seems Celestial Cupcakes' Romeo and Juliet romance is experiencing a sparkle. Kwezi went home to Granny, who turned out not to be a wolf-racist in disguise but just a normal old woman. Nevertheless, she did pull him aside for a moment to ask him if it was true what they said about black men. Kwezi related this to Rakel in a shocked voice. Poor boy. But the real potential monster-in-law was Bonny's father. He shook hands with Kwezi courteously and then excused himself even more graciously and left for his bedroom. From where he never emerged again. It was left to granny-wolf and Bonny's mother to make small talk.

I listen to Kwezi tell Rakel his woes about the evening, and I hear her advice, and see her patting him, and I want to unburden myself to her as if she were a Dear Abby. Dear Rakel-Abby,

I'm married to two men at the same time and it's a bit tricky. Can you give me some advice? I go back to minding my own business, decorating cupcakes in the shape of tiny white and black soccer balls.

Mum contacted me today, after a long silence. She's back from the lakes and wants to know how I am. She says she may stay on longer, through the Canadian summer, into late September. She and Sara might even visit Zuhra, at her invitation. "That's nice," I say. But I'm surprised. Okay, I'm shocked that Mum won't be here for the anniversary of your disappearance, Amal. Aren't you? Does this mean she's letting go? I'm almost happy for her, but I can't help feeling a little sick. Has she forgotten about your anniversary? What will I do on the day?

- You're funny, but wrong. The reason I prefer to avoid my birthday is not because I'm scared of getting old.
- Then what's it about? Have you never had a party?
- Not for years. Not since my sister vanished.

Lately, Bonny has taken to singing around the shop. She's got surprisingly old-fashioned taste in music. It's usually Édith Piaf or Eartha Kitt, sung at the top of her lungs, sometimes even when there are customers present, even though I tell her it's not allowed. After all, we have to have some standards.

Oma liked that kind of music too. Do you remember, Amal, how when we were little she used to change the radio stations until it played the music she liked? Mum would get so cross and tell us to stop fiddling with the radio. Dad, too, in the middle of listening to a rugby match with the commentator sounding like a deranged auctioneer, would suddenly be subjected to the croons of someone like Engelbert Humperdinck. Of course, even if we'd told them it was Oma, they would never have believed us.

Sometimes, the same thing happens in my home. Taj'll be listening to some music and abruptly the CD player will start playing something else, something gentler. And from another part of the house I'll hear those knitting needles clicking away in time to the melody.

– I checked you out on the Internet today.
– Why?
– To see your face.
– And did you see my face?
– No. But I saw the face of a man who bore a remarkable resemblance to you. Perhaps you're related.
– It's possible. So why did you want to see the face of my relative?
– I missed him.
– Shame. Visit him. I have it on good authority that he wants you to.
– Maybe I will.
– You're coming to visit me?
– No, not you. Your relative.

So, Kwezi has taken his beloved to meet his mother. It did not go well. Kwezi's mother (like Bonny's father) made it clear that she didn't like her child's choice of a partner. No, she said, it wasn't about race, it was about dress. Kwezi's mother said Bonny's clothes were "disrespectful and obvious". There was a stand-off, which involved Kwezi getting up and walking off with Bonny clinging to his arm. Now he's even more in love with her than before.

— My mother says hi and that she'd like you to visit her.
— Okay, but this is a bad time. The shop's really busy and Rakel hasn't been well.
— What's wrong with R?
— Nothing specific, just says she's tired all the time.
— Maybe she needs a holiday. You can bring her with you when you visit me. When are you coming?
— Soon.

Barbara and Monica came into the shop today. Rakel had invited them to visit.

At first I didn't recognise them. It was the surprise of seeing them out of context. And together. I wouldn't have thought they'd be friends.

— Your mother called me today. At the shop.
— How is she?
— Fine. She wants me to have supper with your family this weekend.
— Are you going?
— I suppose I must.

- You don't sound too enthusiastic. If you're nervous you can keep me on speakerphone. It will be just like I'm there.
- Sometimes I can't believe we're married.
- Are you regretting it?
- No, but it seems like a dream. Like one of those dreams I have about Amal.

The mornings are freezing as we get closer to winter. Already there have been days filled with black rain. I never used to hate the rain. Or even winter. When I was little I quite liked it. It was a chance to wear red rubber boots and yellow plastic raincoats. Mum would even let us walk in the puddles and not shout at us, except when we forgot to wear those smelly boots.

But then you went away during winter, Amal, and I've never been able to stand the Cape winters since then. But, of course, I've always had to endure them because of Mum. Now, this winter, even Mum's gone. Why aren't I with Darya? What's keeping me here?

Romeo and Juliet walked in today, both subdued. Juliet's period is late.

- Are you reading anything right now?
- Yes, the Qur'an.
- Really? And it's not even Qur'an season.
- When's Qur'an season?
- Fasting month of course.

Are Bonny and Kwezi going to have to get married? Is she going to have an abortion? Will her father ever leave his bedroom? What kind of hair will the baby have? Tune in tomorrow for the next segment in this tragicomedy.

- Come visit.
- Okay.
- Okay?
- Yes, okay. Next month.
- Really? That's amazing!
- Right.
- You don't sound excited?
- I am.
- You don't sound enthusiastic.
- I'm thrilled.
- Are you?
- YES!!!
- Go buy your ticket.

When Bonny does the pee test, the stick records a positive result. Stupid, lucky Bonny. Rakel is practical and makes an appointment for Bonny with Taj's colleague.

- Are you okay?
- Yep, I'm keeping myself busy writing the dreaded memoir.
- I called last night. Your phone was off, where were you?
- Sorry, I was tired so I went to bed early.

- Oh? I thought you were out.
- Don't be silly, where would I go?
- So what do you do when you're not working?
- Nothing much. Domestic duties. Catch up on sleep. Read. Watch TV. Write to you.
- Nothing else?
- Nothing else.

Bonny's pregnancy was a false positive. We wept together, but for different reasons.

- I miss you. I keep imagining I smell the sea and then I think of you.
- The same way whenever I taste or smell vanilla it reminds me of you. It's like I'm under a curse.
- Where have you been tasting vanilla?
- Why? You sound jealous. Are you jealous?
- I told you I don't do jealousy.
- Why have you never asked me about my previous relationships, the girlfriends I had before you?
- Because I'm not the jealous type.
- You could tell me about your ex-boyfriends then.
- I don't have any.
- You're lying.
- I'm not.
- You must have had previous boyfriends.
- There may have been someone but right now I can't believe I was silly enough to get involved with him.

Kwezi and Bonny have broken up. It seems that the thought of almost having a baby with Bonny wasn't a romantic one for Kwezi. Bonny says he told her he wasn't ready to be a father and that their relationship had moved too quickly for him. She says she doesn't mind, rather now than later. So Kwezi's left us for the pizza shop across the road. Rakel says his replacement is going to be a girl.

Amal, I've told Taj I want to go to England on my own. I've been away without him once before, when I visited Cousin Zuhra, so he wasn't too surprised. I've been writing a lot more to Darya recently. But every time I write to him, I know that one day he'll be back, and I'll have to make a decision. I know what I need to do, Amal. It's obvious, isn't it? Even Kwezi, who's younger than me, knows that you can't rush into a relationship and that when you've made a mistake it's necessary to end it decisively. It's not easy making this choice. If I listened to my heart I'd choose to be with Darya. But how can I leave Taj, and what about you, Amal? There've been times recently when it feels as though you're slipping away from me and all I have left is your memory.

Domestic Affairs 101

Tonight the heater has three bars burning and everyone's drinking hot chocolate, including me. I seem to have temporarily lost my taste for cappuccino. Rakel is chatting to Monica and Lucy about the merits of heaters versus actual fires. (I prefer an electric blanket.) Rakel is happy that I'm going away on my own. She says I've seemed so sad recently. I suppose I must have been a bit distant, but the truth is this is the happiest I've felt. At least since you left, Amal.

June is usually a slow month for us at the shop. Not even Father's Day perks it up. So Rakel should be able to cope with just Bonny as backup. We haven't found a replacement for Kwezi yet, and Rakel says she may even close the shop for a week if business is slow.

Alice begins. She says, "Generally, life doesn't make a very good story. It is the relationships we make, the conversations we have, our experiences that give our stories shape. I want you to think specifically about the relationships in your life and, as you write about them, try to identify the patterns."

The women in the class obediently bend their heads over their pages and I hear their pencils and pens scraping away while Alice reads over her notes for the lesson.

What are the patterns in my life? That I'm always second? I am the second daughter of my parents, the second child, Taj's second choice for a bride. I have a second husband who gave me a second-hand wedding ring. In Taj's defence, he did buy me a new engagement ring. But that was because you went missing with the other one, Amal.

I don't think it's possible to see the pattern of your own life until it's over. Are my dreams about you a pattern, Amal? Recently, I've been dreaming about you almost every night. Although I don't always remember the details of the dreams. Sometimes I wake up from one, gasping for air, and as I open my eyes, as my lids lift, I imagine I see you in a shadowy corner of the room, already vanishing, because you've been waiting for me for too long. Is that figure you? Why do you never talk to me? Why don't you wait until I'm properly awake?

Last night, in my dream, you and I were in Paris. I know this because the Eiffel Tower loomed over us. (Yes, I am aware of the Freudian connotations.) We were seated in its shadow, immersed in foamy bath water. Not in a jacuzzi, but a bubble-filled free-standing Victorian bath, claws and all. Although we were sitting in the bath's tepid water, we were still fully clothed in long summer frocks. The dresses were dark and translucent because they were heavy with water. My fingertips were wrinkled. We were both munching on soggy croissants. Mine had an almond filling. Yours was chocolate coated.

Do you know we're eating a symbol of Islam? you asked me.

I said, *I thought it was a symbol of the moon.*

That too, but first it was a symbol of Diana, the huntress, the pagan goddess whose followers took their symbol with them when they switched to Islam. And today Islam is the second largest faith in France, after Catholicism.

It's clear you're Mum's daughter, you both love statistics.

Now, in Alice's class the aroma of the buttery croissant lingers in my nostrils and I begin to salivate. I'm going to have to see if the coffee shop downstairs has any pastries left over before the end of class.

Barbara, the anti-apartheid activist, offers to read.

My mother and father shake their heads at me despondently.

No. No.

They are determined. They are making a joint decision. They are supporting each other in front of me, the child.

I tell them I'll look after this one myself. It will be my responsibility.

No. No.

They say I spend too much time on errands when I should be playing or running around or doing my homework.

I plead. I show them the pools of his eyes, his scratchy whiskers, his fat paws, one egg white, one chocolate brown.

No. No.

They remind me. We have seven dogs and we're living in a three-roomed house.

"But," I beg them, "you have to help him! What's going to happen to him otherwise?"

No. No.

They say there is no money to feed another dog.

If we don't keep him, this little runt dumped on our doorstep will die.

No. No.

They are adamant. They are determined.

So I hide him. After a while he mingles with all the others.

Years later, I have the same thought: If I don't hide this man, he'll be killed.

I'm tired all the time. Maybe I do need a holiday. Part of the reason I'm exhausted is because I toss and turn all night thinking about Darya and my impending visit. It will be the longest time I've spent with him since our brief honeymoon together. I wonder how I'll cope living with a man who isn't Taj.

I've just had my regular "weekend" off, Monday and Tuesday, but I spent most if it reading and napping, apart from a brief spurt of energy when I cleared out a black bag's worth of clothes, mostly the formal suits Shireen bought me in an effort to turn me into a real doctor's wife. Recently Shireen's lost a lot of weight and she's delighted, even though the skin on her face is taut in a parody of youth that makes her look like she's wearing a skull mask. Shireen equates skinniness with youth, so she doesn't eat any food after five in the afternoon, except for sips of hot water with squeezes of lemon. Usually she doesn't even eat from her own plate. She'll just nibble from other people's, especially from Precious's, as though she's his baby.

Mum sent me a bland email saying she's happy, she's thinking of staying longer, have I been round to her house, and how are her herbs.

Yesterday, Taj came home as I was dozing off. He was looking very pleased with himself. He'd bumped into an ex-patient with whose surgery he'd assisted a few years ago. She'd been circumcised as a child. Yes, Amal, I couldn't believe it either. It sounds like something from a horror movie, but it happened right here in Cape Town, back in the late forties, when she was a little girl living in a Muslim community. All her life she'd suffered from vaginal cysts and endless rounds of urinary tract infections. She decided on surgery because she had finally agreed to marry her long-time beau, a step she'd always avoided because of fear of sex. Since the last time Taj had seen her she'd had to endure several more surgeries, but she told him they had been successful. That evening, when Precious came over, I told him her story and he said there was no Qur'anic justification for it. It was a primitive custom from the time of the Pharaohs and was still being practised in certain Muslim communities even today.

Taj is behaving very thoughtfully towards me. I wonder if it's because I'm going away soon. You often hear of couples in arranged marriages like ours, who fall in love with each other, or who claim to fall in love with each other, after they've been married a while. That's never happened with us. Even when he comes home with a harrowing story like he did tonight, there's a reserve in him that makes it seem like I'm a stranger he's meeting for the first time. Even though we've had sex with each other for more than a decade, there's a lack of intimacy between us. I think it's because he couldn't love anyone but you, Amal. Or it could be because I can't have children.

Of course, you never wanted children, did you, Amal? Even when we were little you'd pass on all your dolls to me, and when we were older and you realised it was possible, you said you'd be getting your tubes tied. You even told Taj, one day when he was at our house, soon after his proposal. I remember, he smiled and said something about how you'd already told him your decision several times before, in fact, the very first time you two had met at someone's wedding. He was probably thinking he'd humour you and when you were married he'd soon enough make you see the error of your ways. But I'm sure that as you grew older you would have succumbed to the old tick-tock, tick-tock of your biological destiny.

On the plane to Darya, I finally do some of the homework Alice has set us. We have to write a fictional version of our lives. It feels almost like fun watching my words form, and I enjoy the twisted version of reality I've created. So here's my story, Amal. It's called "Husbandry".

Last night she was with him. This morning, she's mine again.

It's my day off work so I'm an unwilling witness to the bubbling chaos of the children at breakfast. The kitchen's warm domesticity is foreign. I feel as though I've stumbled from bed into someone else's day. She tells me to pour a cup of coffee from the snazzy machine I bought her for our recent anniversary. Instead I decide to empty the dishwasher. I rarely help with household chores. By the time I get home, supper is waiting on the table and most of the kids are in dreamland. What am I trying to prove today? That I can do the housework he disparages?

Memories of the night's meal hug the clean crockery in an invisible cloak as the soft scents of rosemary and coriander drift up from the open dishwasher. I'm not sure where she stores the salad bowls, so I place them in an awkward pile on the counter and turn to see her smiling at me with the indulgent gaze she reserves for the children. She blows me a kiss over their heads. I turn back, reach down for the dinner plates. At least I know where to stack them. The dishes squeak under my fingertips, like shampooed hair. As I pack away her crockery I can hear her chickens squabbling near the backdoor. I collected the newly laid eggs once – again because it was something he'd never do. The hens pecked at my fingers and ankles with cold enthusiasm, in spite of my threats to send them to egg farms where they'd spend their days confined in miniscule coops, tugging out their feathers in mad boredom.

I'm aware of her even as I busy myself with the cutlery. She's combing through the matted hair of the teenage boy who's trying to cultivate an ungroomed look.

The children are scattered around the table the two of us found in an antique store that he suggested we should visit, soon after he'd introduced us.

That first time we met I was cool. She wasn't my type, especially with that mound of preposterous locks. I like women to have sensible hair. Still, she drew my unwilling gaze.

One night, sticky, elongated months after we'd first met, we all went out for dinner. Afterwards he asked me to drive her home. He said he had to get back to the office, some urgent transcontinental call. I'd known him for years; it was a familiar line.

During the drive I felt the light of her eyes on me, weighing me down, making me buoyant. She related an anecdote, some silly story about him, about them. She touched my bare arm to underscore her words, leaving her fingerprints on my skin.

But even as I shrugged off the tattoo of her touch, I could not escape the memory of her eyes, laughing into mine as she chatted effortlessly while my tongue was maple-syrup thick with words I would not speak and fantasies of tasting the skin on the backs of her knees.

It was inevitable. It was right. From the start she told me we'd have to get used to sharing. I had no choice.

This morning I watch her, furtively. Her hair's damp, and she's draped a white towel like a scarf across the shoulders of her red shirt. She's coaxing the children into eating their breakfast, her words as sweet as the badger-friendly honey she drizzles over the porridge to make it palatable to young taste buds. Today, breakfast for the under-sevens is Taystee Wheat made with full-cream milk, slender sticks of sunburnt cinnamon and smooth-as-pebbles blobs of yellow butter. The preteen girls have fairy-sized bowls of organic muesli and cold fat-free milk. The teenage boy has two fried eggs, the yolks like twin orange full moons, with home-baked whole-wheat toast, vegetarian-friendly cheese and tomatoes from the back garden. She's been growing vegetables for years. She even nurtures the sprouts for her salads. She worries about what the children eat, about the food they put in their mouths.

During her first pregnancy, he was mostly absent. I was at her side for the birth. In my mind, I have a photograph of her, flushed and sweaty after the labour, a smear of dried blood in the shape of Italy on her right cheekbone, her scarf askew, black tendrils escaping, gazing in rapture at that child, the fingers of its right hand curled around her wedding band.

That first afternoon back from the hospital, we settled the baby into its hand-me-down crib. Then, while the many relatives took measure of its limbs, the texture of its hair, the colouring of its skin, we went out to the garden. She carried an old ice-cream tub from which green shoots peeped. I carried a shovel and the opaque plastic envelope into which the nurse had reluctantly shoved the placenta and umbilical cord. She'd told me neonatal nurses supplemented their income by selling placentas to cosmetic companies. God, the things women will smear on their faces.

I thought she'd choose a burial corner under one of the weathered oaks in the front garden but instead she picked a shady spot near the log she used as a bench. She sat down gingerly – the stitches she'd acquired during the birth made her movements slow – and directed my digging. I worked without complaint. When the hole was ready, she poured the afterbirth into it, and asked me to sprinkle a thin layer of soil over the bloody tissue. She laughed at my squeamishness. But it wasn't the tangle of auburn blood and breachable membrane that made me queasy, nor was it the rusty scent that reminded me of twisted nails facing upwards, waiting for the yielding fleshy foot of a toddler. It was the gritty sand that I felt with my fingers but could taste in my teeth. When I was little, my mother used to try to convince me to help with the household chores by telling me that one day I'd pick up sand and the grains would turn into diamonds. To test this theory I did pick up sand, and it turned into an oily, plump worm. Now even beach sand makes me seasick.

She knelt cautiously and began to replant the tiny emerald shoots, telling me they were called birds of paradise. She said they were evergreen, that they'd bloom through late autumn and winter, perhaps even into spring. As I watched her slow movements and listened to her words I pictured the sheath from which the flowers would materialise, floral birds' heads with orange and indigo petals. The colours of the dress she was wearing the first time we made love.

Afterwards, while the family argued about whose nose the baby had, we shared a moment of seclusion in the bathroom. She scrubbed my nails with a brush, and soaped my palms before drying them with one of the baby's fresh towels and massaging moisturiser into my skin.

Hoot! Hoot! Hoot! What sounds like a malevolent owl is the arrival of the children's school lift. Kisses are swiftly exchanged. I hear her shut the heavy front door behind the last little body. I begin to pour coffee, and she comes up behind me, hugging me close with her right arm. Waist to waist, we fit snugly into each other's bodies, previously lost pieces of a jigsaw puzzle reunited. The towel lands on the marble floor with a gentle swish as her left hand cups my breast. Her thumb strokes my impatient nipple. I turn to embrace her and we kiss. My lover, my co-wife.

I catch sight of Darya, and it's like the first time again, though this time I can't see his nails because his fingers are clutching a bunch of pink flowers. He stands waiting, his eyes scanning the crowds, searching for mine, and, Amal, the sight of him makes me feel giddy, like that time when we were children and you pushed me too fast on the roundabout.

"Hi," he smiles.

The soles of my feet begin to tingle.

"Hello," I say.

I feel a strange pulse beating in my throat, under my left ear. On the plane over, I kept imagining this moment, our reunion, but now I'm tongue-tied and awkward and the handle of my bag keeps slipping from my hand. He takes the bag from me, holding my fingers, tugging at them until we're holding each other and then I find myself weeping in his arms.

"You're supposed to cry when you leave," he says, holding me closer, "not when you see me."

That makes me cry even harder. I'm not sure if I'm crying for myself, or for you, Amal, or for Taj, or even for Darya. I can't believe I'm here with him, and I can't believe I married him. Under his fingertips my tears stop and I decide right there and then that when I get home I'm leaving Taj.

We make our way to his off-campus accommodation in a warm, punctual train. Darya's studio flat (he says his students call it a posh bedsit) overlooks the canals. There are two walls of windows that offer him glorious views of water and boats and shops and pubs and people walking to and fro, browsing, eating, sending up a hum through the open window that competes with the sound of buskers. It's a huge room, the walls decorated with splashes of framed colour (not mine, he says) and functional, modern furniture. The bed is hidden behind a curtain, pushed up against a window without bars. I climb onto it and crawl across its width to look out the window. I feel as though I've fallen into one of those dreams in which you star so prominently, Amal. Water, water everywhere.

"Where do you paint?" I ask, crawling away from that dizzying window, off the bed and away from him. How am I going to share this tiny space with him, my husband, a man I know so little about?

"My studio's upstairs. I've also got a space on campus. Remember, I'm the resident artist."

"Mmm! You have a title, nice." I walk within range of him. He has that chemical smell around him, and it makes me feel a little high, like I'm glue-sniffing. Hey, Amal, remember the fun we had sniffing Bostik when we did our school projects? Who knew it was also a druggie pastime.

"Thank you," he says, then wrinkles his nose. "Maybe you should take a shower."

"Why? Do I smell?"

"Yes, but I really just want to see you without clothes."

"I'd prefer to shower sans a spectator."

"You're boring."

"And hungry."

"I've got pasta as well as a salad."

"You cooked!"

"No, I bought."

"Wonderful. Let me get clean."

He shows me the way to the bathroom, as if his flat is large enough for me to get lost in it.

The bathroom door locks with a satisfying double click, but then I feel strangely lonely without Darya, as though I've entered a new world, albeit a miniature one filled with towels and without a window. As I stand on the slightly grainy blue tiles washing away the flight's grime it occurs to me that I may never come clean again. What the hell am I going to do? How can I leave the husband who is my last link to you, Amal? But if I stay with Taj, I'll be stuck forever living the life you left behind.

I am momentarily overwhelmed by self-pity, which is stupid. Darya is the one to be pitied, having married a deceitful person like me. Maybe after all these years of living with Taj, I've become like him. I don't want to think about it. What would happen if I came out of the bathroom and told Darya everything, unburdened my heart and soul? What if he said he still loved me, and we could find a way to work things out? What if he told me he never wanted to see me again?

I emerge from the bathroom as clean as I can be, wearing an opaque cotton nightie and with my wet hair in a plait.

Darya says, "You look good." His smile makes my feet burn.

I pretend not to notice the look in his eyes. I'm still half-involved with my inner debate but, more than that, I'm weirdly nervous, as though we haven't slept together before. It's way too late to have an attack of conscience now, Amal, but I know that what I'm feeling is guilt.

The salad dressing is heavy with garlic and a herb I don't recognise. I don't like it, but I move the lettuce around on the plate so it looks as though I'm eating.

I ask Darya to tell me more about the neighbourhood he's living in and he says the entire area has been renovated recently. What was once a no-go part of the city is now trendy, filled with quaint pubs and closet-sized designer boutiques. He says he'll take me out the next day and show me around the shops, libraries, museums and theatres so that I can visit these places on my own while he's at work.

"And I have to show you the ducks. We can feed them this bread if there's any left over."

The pasta he's bought is covered in a heavy chilli and tomato sauce and tastes much better than the salad.

"Although I have to warn you they're pretty belligerent," he says. "Actually, there's one that reminds me a lot of you."

"Charming."

"Those ducks are more likely to rip a chunk of bread out of your hand than to wait around for you to throw them a few crumbs. We must take a trip out on the canal tomorrow – it's the only day I have off this week, so we need to do as much as we can."

"I didn't really come here to see the sights."

"No?"

"I'd rather just look at you."

"You'll get bored soon."

"I'd like to experience that kind of tedium."

"Why? So you can stop missing me?"

"Exactly."

"I never want you to stop missing me. Come here, I'll work on being monotonous."

Much later, I sink into sleep, sniffing his skin, and from my throne of pillows (he remembered I like to sleep with three and has bought some new ones) I watch the lights out on the canal, twinkling and wavering like candle flames. I sleep better than I have in a long time.

The next morning he takes me on the canal in a ferry (or perhaps it's a barge, Amal). I imagine all the creatures in the water below, microscopically sized, swimming under me, while above them I sway on the deck as the vessel does its dance with the others on the water. We pass red-bricked factories that are yesterday's mills and breweries and that today have been turned into snazzy loft-homes for artists like Darya, or people with important jobs in the city. I see a sign for cupcakes and tell Darya we have to check out this distant competition later.

The barge travels under numerous pretty arched pedestrian

bridges, linking people and places, like the connections of a jigsaw, to each other. I enjoy the brief respite from the sun as we go under the bridges and walkways, but the smell in those spaces, soft and wet, makes me think of a dank grave. I suppose you are always in my thoughts, Amal. Even on a warm day in a foreign country I worry that wherever you are, you're cold. And buried somewhere.

We see those ducks that Darya told me about. They squawk and quack along the walks, with their breasts puffed out, like hookers displaying their wares, and use quick eye movements to see if we're offering them treats. They wait on guard, moving one webbed foot up, pushing the other down, weighing our potential as clients. Some of the fiercer ones come right up to the boat, demanding food. A man in blue shorts jogs by, sweat dripping from his nose. A toddler in wellies clumps along heavily from one evaporating puddle to another and, behind him, his mother pushes an empty stroller. Everywhere people are seated at outdoor cafés. I hear the tinkling of their glasses, and the scent of their coffees touches us briefly as we glide by.

By the time our trip is over I'm starving, and Darya takes me to a shop specialising in breads and cheeses. After lunch, as we're walking back to his flat, we see a hairdresser's called Raspberry Hair. I wonder how Jalebi's doing, and the thought of her makes my stomach tense with guilt, but she gives me the courage to do something I've been contemplating for a while. I tell Darya I want a haircut and he whips me inside the door.

(He didn't have to be that enthusiastic.) An hour later, I walk out. My neck feels exposed, but I feel light as a bubble.

"I'm glad you didn't colour it," he says. "I like the silver, it looks like you've plaited tinsel in between your black strands." I smile back at him but, of course, now I'm worried, Amal, that you won't recognise me.

The next morning, Darya's gone when I wake up. He's left a goodbye note on the once-white pillow cover, now stained with my lipstick. I put my lips to each of his xs in turn, snuggle deeper into the bed and my mound of pillows, and pull the duvet up over my eyes, until the sun's rays through the unclothed windows pierce even that protection. I force myself to get up and shower before I venture out into the world where I sink ungracefully into the nearest chair of the closest café, which is actually just outside Darya's building's front door. After a vegetarian meal, I wonder if there are any halaal places around in this fashionable part of town. If they exist anywhere, it should be in this multi-cultural area. I don't think I've ever seen this many races in such a small space. Black, brown, yellow with a hint of cream, Chinese, Greek, Italian, Indian and Pakistani, and, everywhere, children in mini combinations and variations of their parents. Everyone seems tolerant and accepting of each other, but that can't be the whole truth, Amal. I'm sure you remember our distant relatives who live around here somewhere, who still wear saris and are still expected to marry within their "village".

That night, Darya and I go to the movies where we sit co-cooned in the soft, strawberry-coloured leather seats of a theatre named after a screen goddess of yesteryear. The movie is one of those romantic French ones (lots of sex and somebody dies at the end), but what I enjoy best of all is the carrot cake (popcorn's not allowed to stink up the artistic atmosphere), brought to our seat by a smiling server. After the film, we've been invited to a club with Darya's colleagues from work, but once the movie is finished, Darya's not in the mood for other people and I'm not in the mood for too-loud music.

The next time Darya's off work, we go to the local botanical gardens. He wants to have a look at the artwork on display, something about the textures of landscapes in the gardens, and I want to sample the delights of the tea room, scones and clotted cream. I may even have a cupcake or two. Purely for purposes of research, of course.

But first he makes me exercise by going for a walk around the garden. We have a heated discussion about the bonsais. He thinks the trees are attractive works of art. I see them as abused flora and think the practice should be outlawed. I tell him it's like torturing babies: break off an arm here, a bit of leg there, so you can stunt their growth. He tells me I'm crazy. Maybe, but each time I look at one of the plants I can't help but think of pain.

Darya says he's been saving the best for last and takes me to see a vanilla orchid. It is creamy with drops of magenta, like bright freckles on the velvety cheek of a young child. He takes out a sketch he's been working on: in the foreground is an orchid like the one in front of me, and in the background is your face, Amal. You're smiling. Your eyes shine up at me from the page, filled with stories and joy. I'm shaken.

"How did you know what she looks like?" I'm filled with dread. Has he been going through my purse? Did he find that picture of us taken at the Halloween party? Does he know about Taj?

"What who looks like?"

"My sister."

He says, "It's not your sister, it's you. I've never seen your sister."

He looks perplexed. He settles me next to him on a bench in front of the orchid, and begins a new drawing. I look down at the half-finished sketch that's still in my hand.

That's me? That's how he sees me?

He says, "Maybe you and your sister looked alike."

I shake my head. No.

"Don't move," he says.

I look at the picture again, ignoring Darya's moan because I've moved. We were dissimilar in life, Amal, but perhaps now that you're dead I've grown to look more like you. Maybe when I married Taj in your place my face started mutating to look like yours. Or it could be that my eyesight is worsening – I can't remember when last I went for an eye test. Or maybe I'm going nuts.

I stare down at the sketch on my lap (Darya sighs impatiently) and examine it closely. After a while, your face fades, and I see myself, then you reappear smiling, always smiling at me. Maybe we do look alike, but it's only Darya who can see this, and he's brought you alive again through his drawing of me.

Later, to reward my sitting still for an hour (a long, mind-numbing, hour), Darya takes me to the jewellery quarter to choose a gift, a ring, he says, because he thinks I need one of my own along with the one that belonged to his mum. I tell him that I have crow blood and he's going to be sorry if sets me free in a place filled with jewellery, because I like hoarding rings, but he says he's prepared to take the chance. I tell him it's not necessary to get me a new ring, but he says I should think of this one as an anniversary ring. We've know each other exactly four months.

We stroll through the stores along with other couples buying engagement rings. I find hundreds, literally hundreds of rings that I love and want to adopt but, finally, I settle for a teardrop-shaped diamond that slides onto my finger like we were meant for each other. Of course I can't let Darya know about the dozens of rings I have, courtesy of Taj, in my velvety collection back home. You see, Amal, Taj usually buys me a piece of jewellery after one of his indiscretions. I also can't tell Darya that much as I love shiny things, I prefer to keep them in their coffin-like containers. I like to play with them more than I like to wear them. I suppose it's because they remind me too much of you, Amal. You were always the one who enjoyed wearing layers of jewellery, especially rings. But, also, it's impractical to bake or even decorate cupcakes wearing rings. When I first started working for Rakel a ring slid off my fingers into the cupcake batter I was making. Fifteen dozen baked and creatively decorated cupcakes (lions, cheetahs, leopards, tigers) had to be crumbled to death until I found that piece of jewellery again.

The next day, after his lectures, I meet Darya at a coffee shop close to the university. He tells me it's a hip post-grad hang-out. I can't imagine that *hip* is the right word to use. Near our table is a man singing American folk songs from the 1960s, his voice softer than the guitar he's strumming. There's a woman reading Tarot cards in a corner and a group of people arguing (voices only slightly raised) about a recently released popular novel whose author died violently. In another corner, there's a meeting of a knitting club. I imagine I see Oma sitting with them, endlessly knitting those socks of hers. I wonder if she knits socks because her feet are always cold.

After our coffee, I tell Darya I need to visit some bookshops, but he says he wants to take me to see an art museum he loves. My eyelids flutter with boredom. I realise I have to do a lot of reading up on art if there's to be a future with this man but, of course, there isn't. I'm married. To someone else. Every day I wonder if this may be the day he finds out about Taj and leaves me, the way you did, Amal.

One night I'm lying in bed watching the shimmering lights (I've grown very fond of this view, I'm going to miss it as much as Darya) and it occurs to me that we were at the same university at the same time. He tells me he used to come up to the main campus for his language and history lectures. We could have met then. Not that I would have noticed him. I was shrouded in my just-married sign, and, Amal, I was grieving for you. We could have touched the same things at the same time (a bottle of water in the university cafeteria) and I wouldn't have taken him in.

Perhaps we missed each other by moments: I turned a corner, he bent down to tie a shoelace, he smiled at me, I looked behind him at a girl whose hair was cut in the style you wore the day you disappeared. Even if our fingers had grazed over that water bottle, I would have felt nothing, asleep as I was, the kind of slumber that not even a fairytale kiss can disturb.

One dark night, close to my departure, I wake up and Darya's not with me. Alone now, I remember my other husband, my other life. There've been a couple of emails from Taj and Precious to which I responded briefly, with the kind of guilt I never imagined I'd feel.

I can guess where Darya's gone: upstairs to his top-floor studio, where he's been sneaking off to work on his new collection. I pull on a jersey over the new nightie he bought me (a silky, near transparent, mostly useless thing) and go to find him. The first thing I experience whenever I'm in his studio is the noise, despite the silence. In my head I hear the crash of surf from the photographs and half-finished paintings that litter the walls and floor like the ocean's debris washed ashore.

Some of Darya's canvasses are huge structures, six feet high, eight feet tall; others can fit on a small easel. With the big pictures he uses palette knives, sponges, rags, his hands, those fingers with their stained fingernails that I love. A painting can take up to a year to dry, sometimes less, sometimes longer, depending on how many layers are involved. He uses linseed oil to make his oil paints more fluid, glossier. That was the creamy chemical smell I noticed hanging around him when we met in the lift.

I recognise some of the photographs he took on our honeymoon. Although Mum's sea isn't always visible, I am present in several of the photos. It's strange to see myself from different angles, my face lit, or in shadow. Looking like you, Amal. There's no escaping that now.

In Darya's photographs of Mum's sea there are shifting flashes of light lying like small gold coins thrown onto the always moving water, the physical and mythical meeting place of oceans and ghosts and gods.

There are several huge canvasses leaning against the walls, some with their backs to me, others in various states of incompletion. Darya seems to be working on a few pieces simultaneously. There's a charcoal sketch of a rock waiting for a breaker to smash into it, and an almost complete seascape, overshadowed by the ambers of sunrise or dusk. Another displays soft wet sand contrasting with the harshness of dark rock.

I never thought you could dissect something like the liquid particles of a wave, that a single breaker could be painted in the tiniest of drops. Before I knew Darya, I never noticed the contrast in the colours of the foam floating on the sea. The coloured edges and the different tones of shadows, like the cells of human skin.

Now I watch him painting debris: it floats on the surface of a patchwork sea quilt. A lighthouse, impassive, judges the waters with its searching beams. He uses his fingers to smooth out the colour, to provide additional mist, a touch of watery softness. I see him wipe off a section of the work and leave it to dry to paint over it later.

"Hello," I interrupt, and he turns to smile at me, without really seeing me. "I thought you said you weren't going to paint with your fingers anymore." Much as I love his stained fingers, Darya has told me that direct contact with the paint can be dangerous.

"I know, but sometimes I have to let my fingers communicate with the paint directly or I feel too removed from the painting."

"As long as you remember to clean them properly."

Yes, I'm thinking of Taj.

"I promise I will."

"What are you doing now?"

"I'm working on shading to bring a bit of realism to this rock. You see, everything real needs a shadow."

Then I must be doubly real, Amal. I have a shadow and you. Now I watch in fascination as he forms bubbles in the spray. He draws a dark line under the foam.

"Why are you doing that?" I ask.

"To give it more dimensionality," he says.

The bubbles float off the canvas, sparkling in a patch of sun.

"They look real."

I'm amazed that a few globs of white paint can give the impression of sunlight.

He says, "That's good, I'm glad you think so. That's the challenge, to bring the sea to life, to bring movement to the curl of a wave and show the shape and patterns of that movement."

Alice would like him.

I look at the half-finished paintings, hear the screech of a seagull, feel the hardness of rock under the soft soles of my feet, watch the movement of his wrist as he forms the sky, a hypnotic backwards and forwards flick of sapphire blue.

"How did you begin this?" I point to the painting he's busy with now.

"I started from a charcoal sketch." As he talks to me he continues to work on the painting, gesturing with his thumb when he wants me to look at something in particular. "It's difficult sometimes getting the rocks right. You don't want them to look as though they're sitting on top of the water. It has to seem like the water is playing at the bottom of the rocks."

He's talking to me, but he's forgotten I'm here. He paints, dips his brush in water, wipes it on a roll of paper towel, takes paint directly from cans. A splash of black shapes itself into a rock. It's more magical than watching flour and eggs become cupcakes.

I turn away from him and notice a painting that's leaning against the wall. There's a figure sitting on a rock, well out to sea, long hair blowing in the wind.

"Who's that?" I ask.

"A mermaid. I put her in especially for you."

"For me? Why?"

"Because you told me that you found the story about the mermaid who loses her tongue depressing. That it made you sad when you were little. But here she is, and you can see she's alive and happy."

The mythical figure has both her arms raised to the dawn, welcoming the light.

"Why did the story make you sad?" says Darya.

"She was in love with a prince who was two-timing her. And even though she sacrificed her tongue, he married someone else."

"Rotten prince."

"I wonder how he'd feel if she'd been deceiving him with another man," I say. Why am I doing this? I hear the fury of breakers, taste my fear as I swim out to shelter behind a painted boulder.

"I don't think the prince would mind if there was another guy, as as long as she didn't love that other man," says Darya.

The roar in my ear recedes, my breathing stills.

"Would you like to paint something?"

He motions me to an easel, shows me some tubes of paint, turns back to his work. I pick up a paintbrush, squeeze out the tubes of colours he's offered and stare at the canvas. It reminds me of my first writing moment with Alice, a void that I'm supposed to fill, only now using a brush instead of a pen. Except I understand the mysterious language of art even less than I understand the idiom of words. I squeeze red and pink onto the board. Dab the paint with my fingers – it's surprisingly cold. Then I spread the colours over the canvas with brush and sponge and, when I'm done, there are my familiar frilly-tailed kites and balloons with long strings attached. They've flown back to me from undergraduate doodling days.

He glances over his shoulder at me and says, "Not bad. For a three-year-old."

"Thank you. I hope you don't speak to your students like that."

"I don't really teach my students. They're at a stage where they're developing a personal style. They aren't meant to emulate me, I'm guiding them along the path, that's all."

He adds, "I like watching you paint, it's sexy. Come here."

"Nope, you're interrupting my delicate creative process." But I put down my brush with feigned reluctance.

He gets to me before I reach him, pulls me into an embrace, and the linseed oil perfumes our lovemaking on the paint-splattered wooden floor, the half-finished seas looming above us, benign or malevolent, depending on the angle of your eye.

Turning Tears into Diamonds

I think of Darya when I look out of Alice's window at the sea below. This evening it's opaque, an agitated cauldron, and I half expect a mythical sea monster to rise from its churning depths, demanding a human sacrifice. I'm sure Darya would be interested in painting this liquid mass below me.

Lucy is knitting, with two needles (she's obviously not as gifted as Oma), and explaining the intricacies of her work to Rakel. I hope Rakel doesn't make us take up knitting after this, seeing as tonight's our last writing class. The next time we see Alice it will be to hand over our final manuscripts. Tonight we're having a party. I've brought book-shaped cupcakes, and there are cheeses and dips and plenty of drinks.

Alice begins our last lesson.

"In the process of writing our story, we remember our pasts, we collect our scattered memories and reawaken our stories. Tonight, I want you to write about something that happened in your life, and which, at the time, may have seemed insignificant, until you got a chance to re-examine it."

Alice begins to wind her pesky timer and, as usual, everyone begins to write without pause. It's July, the month of your vanishing. It's been almost twelve years since you came into my bedroom that chilly winter morning, since you woke me up while you searched for that jersey of mine you wanted to borrow. It has been almost twelve years since you and I last touched. I begin to write.

Later, at our end-of-class party, I eat more than I should, thinking about what I'd written and couldn't read to the rest of the class. Everyone hugs goodbye and makes vague promises to meet. Rakel says she'll invite the class to the shop for a celebration after we've all completed our manuscripts.

When I drive Rakel home, the False Bay coast hisses water at us for as long as we are within spitting range. I wonder if it's in cahoots with Darya, forcing me to remember him. Darya is insistent that I return to England. The university has invited him to stay on for a second semester. He wants me to join him until the end of his stay. He says he's sure Rakel will understand. After all, we are married. Of course he doesn't realise I haven't told Rakel about our marriage. At the very least, he wants me to visit him in August, even if it's only a brief visit.

Sometimes I feel like succumbing. Other times I wonder why he takes it for granted that I'll give up my work, my business for him. Maybe he doesn't consider what I do as being as worthy as his career.

- Are you okay?
- Yep. I'm finishing up my memoir. Although I don't feel all that cap-
  able of writing today. I feel inept.
- All part of the creative process, those moments when you feel
  useless.
- So how do you get over it?
- Leave the work alone and go for a walk.
- I can't, I have a deadline.
- Then write a story about me.
- Thanks, maybe I will.
- I miss you.
- Me too.

Tonight there's a dinner party that Taj, Precious and I have
to attend at Shireen's house, but as we're leaving for it my
head begins to pound and my skin is covered in a fine mist
of sweat. Taj says I must be getting the flu and helps me into
bed. Even though I feel awful, part of me is glad I won't have
to see Shireen.

I dream I hear you softly laughing, Amal, and then your
chortle turns into a hiccough that sounds like a sob. I wake up.
Taj is in bed, having a nightmare. I shake him awake and he
looks at me in confusion. "I was dreaming about Amal." We
say those words simultaneously. We stare at each other.

He says, "I'll make us something to drink."

I wait for a few minutes, breathing shallowly, then after a
while I fall asleep. Later, when I wake up, there's a cup of cocoa

on my bedside table, a thin layer of milky brown skin congealed on its surface. I hate cocoa.

I go back to sleep after taking something for my throbbing head. I hope the pill will also help with the pain in my stomach. It's early, but I call Rakel and tell her I have flu and that I won't be in for the day. She mutters words of commiseration. I sleep. Only to wake up to the sound of woodpeckers drilling their way out of my brain.

But, no, it's Precious knocking at our closed bedroom door. I pull the duvet up to my chin and pretend to be dead, clutching as many pillows as I can find to my side.

"Go away, I'm sick," I tell Precious when he walks in, despite his knock being unanswered.

I know what Precious is here to tell me. Last night I saw the signs. He's at the beginning of another religious cycle. Today he's wearing a long kurta and topee (not to be confused with a toupee, which I swear our father has taken to wearing recently, Amal). In case I don't notice his attire, he solemnly greets me with Assalamu Alaikum wa Rahmatullahi wa Barakatuh. "My sister," he adds.

I grunt a response. Precious hasn't had a religious phase for a while now, not since he acquired Jalebi. Usually there'll be months of dagga-smoking, followed by at least two weeks of pious praying and attending university lectures.

"My sister in Islam …"

"Jesus loves you."

Do you remember, Amal, when we were children, the first

time we saw those words written in the sky by a clever plane? We thought it was a direct message from God to little Christian boys and girls.

"Taubah, taubah!" exclaims my freshly religious neighbour. He moves his hand from one side of his mouth to the other three times, shaking his head sadly at me, his mouth turned down like the sad clown from that circus Dad forced us to go to year after dull year when we were kids.

"My sister, I am off to study in the sacred mosque."

"Cool."

"Yes, Malak, it is nearing our holy month and I must make plans to be closer to our Creator."

"I can't take you seriously when you're wearing a dress, Precious. Besides, fasting isn't for a while."

"One can never begin too early. I shall make dua for you my sister. For you and my brother, that Allah paak will bless you with many sons."

"Don't you dare." I sit up and, even though the right side of my head experiences a spasm of pain, like it's been hit by a lightning bolt, I manage to throw one of my pillows at him.

"My sister …"

"If you do, I'll make dua your mother finds out about Jalebi."

"Jalebi." He says her name like she's recently deceased. "That is what I'm here to tell you. I've left Jalebi in Taj's study."

"Why?"

He looks down.

"I cannot have her in my home. She is napaak."

"Now she's dirty? You didn't think she was dirty when you chose that ridiculous hair colour or paid for her."

"I'm hoping my duas will be answered and I can leave her behind."

"What's wrong with her behind? You chose it. And her other body parts. And her thigh-high leather boots and that ridiculous skirt."

I see his expression turn inwards with the memory of her outfit.

"I have to go," he mutters, and leaves.

A noise from behind me makes me realise Taj has been awake through this whole exchange. I'm so used to his absence that having him in bed is a surprise.

"You're too hard on him."

I get out of bed to search for headache pills, only to be pulled back into Taj's arms. It seems he likes the images conjured up by those boots and that skirt. There have been times in our marriage when I've felt moments of desire for Taj, but this is not one of them, and I push him away.

What am I going to do? There must be a light at the end of this tunnel I'm in. I'm sure I can see glimmers of it. I only hope it's not the light from the fires of hell. Tomorrow is the anniversary of your disappearance, Amal.

I fall asleep again and immediately sink into a dream about you. We're in the middle of Cousin Zuhra's man-made lake, the one near her house, floating on rubber alligators in that faraway land, and all around us live alligators of various sizes are floating too, but we're too hot to care. You smile like a cat, a neat smile that doesn't spread across your face. Your nose doesn't wrinkle. You say, *Malak, you're the only one who should care. Alligators can't harm me. I'm dead.*

I push myself up on an elbow to look at you, to make sure you're real. It's always good to see you, even though, this time, I'm aware it's a dream and I'm going to wake up and you're still going to be missing. Your fingers trail in the clear water, and a decoy duck drifts by with a places-to-go-people-to-see expression in its painted eyes.

Why'd you marry him?

I thought it was a way of making sure you were dead.

What?

I thought that if you were alive, you'd be sure to come back. It was the one way I had of ensuring that you'd come back.

You thought if I were alive I'd appear in time to stop the wedding? Like that book? Like that mad woman's brother in your favourite book?

Exactly.

You're a fool. Do you love him?

No, don't be silly. He's your boyfriend.

You smile at me and I see the sparkle in your eyes. You blow me a spit-bubble kiss.

I wake up in my bed, alone, feverish, my brain dense like peanut butter. My body feels heavy outside of the water, heavy with remembrances, heavy with homesickness for you, Amal, for Mum, for Darya. It's mid-afternoon. I stumble to the bal-

cony but, when I open the door, the brutal wind rushes the
curtains into my face, enveloping my body in their fabric, like
a shroud. I shut the door, but I can still hear the call to prayer,
like the cry of an abandoned baby. It's Precious playing the
azan repetitively on his CD player, as a way of exorcising his
demons.

The medicine cabinet yields very little to help me with my
head (so much for being married to a doctor), but I find a packet
of effervescent vitamin Cs and wait impatiently for three to dis-
solve in a glass of water. I'm going to have to find a real doctor
to go to today.

I turn on my computer and hear the ribbit of the frog-
croak that announces a new email. The subject reads "Come
Back" and I feel the tears on my face. I don't know why I'm
weepy today. Trailing over the square letters of my keyboard
is a small white hair. I pick it up, sniff at it, imagine the smell
of cloves. My chest feels like an unwashed concrete floor,
every breath I take is thick with dust. Outside I hear the wind
howling. I can't go to the pharmacy, so I decide to rummage
through Taj's office: on a previous occasion I found free drugs
samples, handed to him by medical reps, not too long past
their sell-by-date.

Usually I don't bother to go into Taj's office, not even to
kill dust motes. It's his sanctuary. For a moment I think I have
stepped into Bluebeard's chamber (Cousin Zuhra on the brain)
because as I open the door the first thing I see is a dead woman.
Then I realise it's Jalebi. She's seated on the couch, dressed in a

demure black skirt, showing her knees, but no thigh flesh, and a matching long-sleeved blouse. Something is very wrong. Her head is on the couch next to her, lying there like a handbag, her mouth wide open in a pornographic pout, her mouldy violet eyes smiling. Precious has decapitated her.

I suppose he means to show me how serious he is about his latest new leaf.

Poor Jalebi. I was there at her conception, and I am saddened by her death. I feel yet another shower of tears prickling warmly at the corners of my eyes. What the hell's wrong with me today? Something crawls out of Jalebi's headless cleavage and scuttles off. I scream, even as my brain recognises it as a harmless gecko. I stumble backwards into Taj's desk, causing it to tilt, to topple away from me, until it rests at an unnatural slant against the wall, with his chair trapped between the desk and the wall. I save his laptop as I get the desk upright, but I see the slow slide of the other objects that were on the desk as they tumble to the wooden floor. Pens and pencils bounce and clatter along with a portable phone, and a small bottle of water, half-full and uncapped, sloshes over the whole mess. Shit.

I pull the desk straight and begin mopping up. My hand closes over a pregnant Russian nesting doll, one of the many gifts he gets at fertility symposiums around the world, like the pregnant Barbie with the visible foetus facing downwards. The matryoshka has been on his desk since the early days of our marriage, but I don't think I've looked at her properly. Now she comes apart in my hands and the next doll in the nest is revealed. It feels like I'm unpeeling a pregnant onion. She makes me want to weep again. Perhaps I've broken her. Them. I sit down on the couch next to Jalebi, move her head deferentially into her lap and open the doll to reveal her smaller sisters, one by one, until for the briefest time, everything slows, everything shuts down, even my heartbeat.

The lamp in Taj's office is lit. I'm still in the pjs I wore to bed the night before. The clock on the wall, which is in the shape of a pregnant belly, says it's way past 2 am. Someone is knocking on the front door. My head and body find it hard to cooperate, but eventually I get the door open and peer through my swollen lids. It's the police. Their words don't make sense: something about Taj and a car accident. Dead on impact. Later, someone takes me to bed. I am hot, I am freezing. I sleep in a swirl of black waters where white figures loom.

When I wake up again, my head is clear and I can breathe without hearing the death rattle in my chest. Mum is sitting in one corner of my room sewing and Rakel is snoring gently in another. Mum's dark head is bent over her quilting. Her hand moves gently high and low as she sews in her usual methodical way. Their presence makes me feel safe. I sleep again.

After a couple of weeks, when I am feeling better physically, when I've blunted all the sensations in my head and body, I move out of the house Taj and I have shared. I move to Mum's complex, but not to her home. Heartbreak can only bring you so close. I live in the house of a woman called Elizabeth, who is journeying around the world. I've been finishing this memoir for you, Amal, and, as you can see, it's almost reached its conclusion, but then you've always known how it was going to end.

Sometimes I miss getting up early to bake cupcakes, sometimes I miss the smell of vanilla, but this is my new life, and I can't return to the old one. Oma used to tell us: if your knitting's unravelled, it's time to begin again. I'm beginning again. But before I do, let me go back to that matryoshka in Taj's office.

When I unpack her, I see the impossible. Time stops. Then the nausea that has been threatening me since the night before rises, and I barely make it to the bathroom in time, my body shuddering with each breath. I retch and heave and cough, ripping off my jersey and my pyjama top as my body overheats.

But when my body is empty, when my world has stopped spinning and I am cold enough to reach for my clothes and for water to wash my face, I wonder if I've dreamt it all. I go back to Taj's office. There it lies on the floor with that doll and her small mirror-innards, glittering in the morning's shadows, sparkling as though it hasn't been hidden for years. There has to be a rational explanation.

I spend the afternoon in Taj's study, sleeping intermittently on his couch, waiting for him to come back. I haven't answered the ringing phone and I've heard my computer announce more messages from Darya, but I am numb to him, because he lives in a different space and time.

Taj finds me in his refuge. I show him my discovery. Even in the gloom of dusk it shines, inelegant and gaudy. Shireen must have helped him to choose it.

Taj sinks down behind the safety of his desk. He switches on the lamp. Begins to speak. Stops. Puts his head in his hands, sighs. His shoulders shake. Is he crying? When he looks up at me again, his face is crumpled, like one of the discarded papers that litter the area where I've been sitting writing this last chapter. His lips become thicker, the bottom one is trembling. Does he imagine his tears will move me?

I want to hit him. But I'm afraid that, like Jalebi, I will lose my head if I touch him, so I stay on that couch, mere metres from him, a lifetime away.

He says, "I'm sorry, I'm sorry, I'm sorry."

I have no sympathy.

All these years, he's had your engagement ring on his desk, hiding in that doll. On his desk. Like a souvenir. Do you remember, Amal, how Mum used to hide our birthday presents like that, in our own rooms, where we'd least expect to find them? Did you tell him the secret of hiding in plain sight, Amal?

"Don't be angry, please, let me explain," he says.

"Don't tell me how to feel. How did you get this ring? How did you get the ring that's supposed to be on Amal's missing finger?"

"It came off her finger when she fell."

"What?" It comes out as a screech.

I feel a pounding beginning in the right side of my head, as if my brain is trying to escape my skull rather than stick around to listen to him. He covers his face with his hands again. This is good, because I don't want to see him. But it's also bad, because now he mumbles through his fingers, and I have to strain to hear the words. His confession.

"We'd arranged to meet. That night, after your father had taken his sleeping pill. But I got there late. I was caught up in an emergency at the hospital. It was pointless. The baby and the mother died anyway. I drove to Amal, imagining how she'd comfort me. But she was furious with me because I was late. She'd been waiting in the cold for an hour. Eventually we made up, in my car. It was going to be dawn soon. I needed to drive back to be at the hospital. She got angry with me again. She said the least I could do was watch the sunrise with her. I walked her back towards the tent. We were arguing in that wind, above the noise of the surf. I told her I needed to work, and I tried to take her in my arms again. She pulled back.

"I've played the scene over and over in my head. I've dreamt it again and again. I reach for her. She steps back. And back. Something crumbles under her feet. I reach for her. But all I get is the ring that was always too big for her narrow fingers. She's gone. In an instant. She makes no sound when she falls – I don't even hear her landing.

"I went down to the sea. But even from a distance I knew her body was twisted into an unnatural position. The back of her skull was crushed. She must have bounced on her way down. She was lying face down in the water. The waves were pulling at her, stroking her as I had done minutes before. She was so still, even as the water stirred all around her. When I turned her over, I saw her eyes, open in surprise. I let the sea take her.

"I was selfish. I thought my career, my life, would be ruined. Even if my name was cleared, even if they believed it was an accident. I didn't think of her. I let her go.

"It was an accident. I'd never understood the tragedy of that word. Misfortune and disaster rolled into one word. It was an accident. But I was responsible."

He takes his hands away from his face and looks at me. There's a burst blood vessel in his right eye. Snot as thick as marrow drips from his nostrils.

An accident. You've been dead. All these years, you've really been dead. All these years. When I told myself you were missing, that you had to be dead, I always hoped that I was lying to myself. I hoped there'd be a reunion. You'd had amnesia. You were well looked after. You were safe. All these years. You've been dead. You are. Dead.

Surely it would have been easier to face the immediacy of your death than the torture of not knowing, which we lived with for so long. It would have been easier to know that once you existed, and then you were gone. But instead, for weeks and months, forever afterwards, I'd step into the places we'd gone to together, the library, the sweet shop, and I'd have to endure the same question, asked lightly, "Where's your sister, today?" Foolishly, I always told the truth, my voice croaking. You were missing, I'd say. They'd say sorry. Until I stopped going to our old haunts. It's only now that I realise why Mum needed to move. It must have been so much worse for her. But even in her new home, there was no replacing you.

Taj is standing now, leaning with his back against the open window, and behind his shoulder I see the inky night sky, with a full moon like a single pearl earring looking for its mate. I wonder what colours Darya would use if he were to paint this sky. Taj says he has to go to work. He comes towards me but is stopped by the hand I hold up to ward him off.

He walks away. With his back to me, he says, "You know I love you, don't you?"

"Drop dead," I tell him.

I wished Taj dead. But in reality, there was no convenient car accident. In reality, Taj did not die the night he told me he'd killed you. Instead, he drove off to his bountiful hospital and brought more lives into the world. I suppose that's his way of trying to balance the scales. Kill one Amal, help a few hundred couples conceive.

But his choice of road has led me to mine. I live here quietly, close to Mum, but away from her too. When you grow up, finally, you have to do so on your own. And I need to grow up quickly. There's not much time left, Amal, because you're going to be an aunty soon.

How? you'll ask, if I'm infertile. I'm not. Taj was. Is. I keep hoping my fantasy will come true and that he really dies, so whenever I speak of him I like to do so in the past tense. If he had any decency he'd have killed himself that night he told me about you.

The problem with the pregnancy is that it's left me confused as to what to do about Taj. I've spoken to Koos and told him Taj's story about your death. We've neither of us told Mum, though. Koos says it's up to me to decide. That they may still be able to build a case against Taj. Thing is, although he's proved to be a lying bastard, I believe him about you. I believe your death was an accident. Maybe I'm wrong, but I don't want to put Mum through a court case when she's at her happiest preparing a quilt for her granddaughter. Oh, did I forget to mention you're having a niece?

Long ago, when Taj and I had been married around a year or two (I can't remember exactly), we were at one of those interminable dinner parties of Shireen's, one to which the entire clan was invited. An old aunty of Shireen's came up to Taj and Precious, pinched their cheeks and said the last time she'd seen them they'd both been teenagers, sick in bed with mumps and chicken pox. Taj changed the subject smoothly to the old woman's many ailments (bunions, an ulcer, a heart that needed to be kick-started every so often, like an old car).

I never thought about it again. Not until Rakel's doctor, who diagnosed pneumonia, and had me hospitalised, who kept me in womb-darkness, and kept Taj away from me, while ordering Mum home from Canada, told me I was several months pregnant.

Life can fall apart between breaths, but it can also reconstruct itself in the same space of time.

The doctor allowed Taj in for a visit. I asked him if he was infertile. He told me that both Precious and him had had mumps, but that he'd got a secondary infection, and one of its side effects was infertility.

This time, I made sure he didn't look away when we spoke. I wanted to see his face when I told him I was pregnant. He never asked about the baby's father, just said he'd arrange for the talak. Not that it means anything to me, because he was never free to marry me anyway: he was always your husband, Amal.

I asked Precious if I could keep Jalebi, and she moved with me here to the coast. I fixed her head with lots of heavy-duty adhesive tape and bought her some turtleneck tops to cover her cellophane bandages. She's got a new career as a professional passenger, or as a co-driver if you'd prefer her to sound less passive. Whenever the women in the compound need to drive anywhere late at night, alone, Jalebi goes with them to scare off potential hijackers. She seems content.

Do you remember the last time we spoke, Amal? I wrote about it in class. But I couldn't read it aloud to the others, although I had to give each of them, even Rakel, a copy.

I remember our mother used to call her cherry-pink lipgloss her "smile", and she never went out without wearing it. I remember after my sister vanished, our mother stopped smiling. She took to wearing flavourless, colourless lip balm.

I remember.

My sister wakes me up by barging into my room, switching on

*my overhead light, opening my cupboard and talking to me loudly.
One of the actions is sure to wake me, but all of them simultaneously make me furious.*

"What the hell?"

*I hug my black continental pillow close to my body and snuggle
into the smaller puffy pillow with its white anglaise cover that leaves
wrinkles on my cheeks even after I've been awake for hours.*

*My sister says she wants to borrow my new blue jersey. I mumble
into my pillows that she's crazy, my jersey is at least three sizes too
big for her, but she says it's perfect, she's going to use it over her pjs
in the sleeping bag. I hear the thuds as she throws unwanted clothes
and books onto the floor and her sigh of relief when she finds what
she's looking for.*

*As she leaves, she tugs the duvet off my body, and with it my last
hopes of sleep. She giggles and bangs the door behind her, leaving
the light on. "You cow," I scream at her, struggling to get the bed-
ding off the floor.*

"I love you too," she shouts through the closed door.

"Go to hell," I respond.

*I remember that throughout the exchange I never once looked
at her.*

*I remember that those were the last words I spoke to my sister,
the sister I would never see again. I wish I could take the words back
or, at the very least, I wish I could stop remembering them.*

I can't tell you how sorry I am, Amal. For our last childish argument, for the way you died. Even now, as this foetus develops

inside me, I think of your body, left alone to disintegrate. Life isn't fair.

If you're wondering about Darya, I've told him nothing about Taj, or the pregnancy. It seemed cowardly to do it over the phone or even in an email. Which is why I'm back in the city, waiting for his return.

Last week he sent me photographs of the paintings he'll be exhibiting in England's spring, before he leaves the university. He's almost finished – he's just waiting for the layers to dry.

The paintings are part of a series. The first one begins on the dark ocean floor, showing prawn holes and an assortment of fish, and then the paintings move upward, towards the light of the seashore. The last is of me on Mum's beach, at an imaginary point where the oceans overlap. In the painting, I have two shadows, one for each ocean, one for me and one for you, Amal. He calls the painting "State of Grace".

Perhaps that is what I'm experiencing now, when I get a whiff of Oma, sweet and solid as a cloud, reminding me that I'm not alone. Do people visit graves to remember the dead? If so, then memories need to be visited too. Maybe that's why Mum sews her quilts.

I was looking at your memory-quilt the other day, and I decided that it's not Mum's tears in the borders. They're Oma's diamonds, shielding us. I've learnt to enjoy watching their light, as I wait, for Darya, and, always, for you.

Acknowledgements

My gratitude to:

Fourie Botha, Fahiema Hallam, Frederik de Jager, Carla Potgieter and Sabrina Knipe at Umuzi for their generous support.

Anne Schuster for my box of Awry 101 and for allowing me to utilise *Foolish Delusions* (Jacana, 2005).

Bronwyn McLennan, my brilliant OC editor, for coffee, sympathy and advice followed by tea and books.

Shehaam Appoles, Debbie Ludik, Liz Mackenzie, Maire Fisher and Anne-marie Hendrikz for their cheerful optimism.

Erica Coetzee and Nella Freud for much suffering as first readers.

Nurul-Ayn for bringing light, art and music into the swampland of my mind.

Nuri, my numero uno reader and marketer.

JB for Disney-Dreams.

Gabeba Baderoon for infinite encouragement.

SB for motivating my frivolity.

EN for providing the germ that became *Husbandry*.

For everyone who helped with research, words and ideas, willingly and/or resentfully, my deepest thanks.